W9-ATM-869

"Just Imagine The Perfect Husband," Michael Drake Suggested.

"That's exactly what we try to be. We cater to the executive woman who doesn't have the time or, frankly, the skill to deal with the mundanities of running a home."

Kendra imagined Michael as the perfect husband, and it was both appallingly easy and painfully difficult to do. As diplomatically as possible, she asked, "You don't—er—live in?"

He shook his head firmly. "Strictly against policy. But we are on call twenty-four hours a day. We realize that household emergencies aren't limited to business hours, and we're here to take care of all your needs."

All her needs. Now, that definitely had possibilities. Kendra found herself looking at the man in a whole new light.

His lips quirked at one corner as he effortlessly read her mind, and he clarified, "All your *household* needs."

Dear Reader:

Happy Valentine's Day!

It takes two to tango, and we've declared 1989 as the "Year of the Man" at Silhouette Desire. We're honoring that perfect partner, the magnificent male, the one without whom there would *be* no romance. January marks the beginning of a twelve-month extravaganza spotlighting one book each month as a tribute to the Silhouette Desire hero—our *Man of the Month*!

Created by your favorite authors, these men are utterly irresistible. Joan Hohl's Mr. February is every woman's idea of the perfect Valentine, and March, traditionally the month that "comes in like a lion, goes out like a lamb," brings a hero to match with Jennifer Greene's Mr. March.

Don't let these men get away!

Yours,

Isabel Swift
Senior Editor & Editorial Coordinator

DONNA CARLISLE
A Man Around the House

Silhouette Desire

Published by Silhouette Books New York

America's Publisher of Contemporary Romance

SILHOUETTE BOOKS
300 East 42nd St., New York, N.Y. 10017

Copyright © 1989 by Donna Ball Inc.

All rights reserved. Except for use in any review,
the reproduction or utilization of this work in
whole or in part in any form by any electronic,
mechanical or other means, now known or
hereafter invented, including xerography,
photocopying and recording, or in any information
storage or retrieval system, is forbidden without
the permission of Silhouette Books, 300 E. 42nd St.,
New York, N.Y. 10017

ISBN: 0-373-05476-9

First Silhouette Books printing February 1989

All the characters in this book are fictitious. Any
resemblance to actual persons, living or dead, is
purely coincidental.

®: Trademark used under license and
registered in the United States Patent and
Trademark Office and in other countries.

Printed in the U.S.A.

Books by Donna Carlisle

Silhouette Desire

Under Cover #417
A Man Around the House #476

DONNA CARLISLE

lives in Atlanta, Georgia, with her teenage daughter. Weekends and summers are spent in her rustic north Georgia cabin, where she enjoys hiking, painting and planning her next novel.

Donna has also written under the pseudonyms Rebecca Flanders and Leigh Bristol.

One

There's a squirrel in my fireplace!"

"A what?" On the other end of the telephone line Patty's voice sounded muffled. She was eating, Kendra thought indignantly. How could she eat at a time like this?

"A squirrel!" Kendra practically shouted into the mouthpiece. "Who do you call about getting a squirrel out of your fireplace?" As she spoke, Kendra was franticly flipping through the yellow pages. *Squirrels, removal of.* No listing.

"Well, certainly not me. Where's Maurice?"

"Hiding under the bed, where else?"

"Did you try tuna?"

"Squirrels don't eat tuna! Even I know that!"

"No, for Maurice."

"Good heavens, all I need is that neurotic cat running around loose in a room with a killer squirrel. He's better off where he is. What about the fire department? Do you think if I called the fire department—"

Her words were cut off by the loud clattering and banging of the glass doors that enclosed the fireplace accompanied by the screech of sharp claws against the panel and the high-pitched squeal of a terrified animal. Kendra winced and covered her free ear with her hand as she whirled anxiously toward the family room. "Listen to that! Can you hear that! I can't listen to that noise all night—it's driving me crazy! What am I going to do?"

Patty's long-suffering sigh filtered over the telephone wire. "Go to the kitchen," she advised, "and pour yourself a glass of wine. I'll be right over."

"I never had these problems in my apartment!" was Kendra's parting shot, and she hung up the phone.

Kendra poured a glass of wine and spent the next half hour pacing the length of the family room and muttering to herself. It was not, of course, that Kendra expected Patty to know any more about removing squirrels from fireplaces than she did. But it had been Patty's idea for Kendra to buy the house in the first place, and Kendra felt it only fair that her partner share in some of the hazards of home ownership. Besides, she could definitely use the moral support, and in a case like this it stood to reason that two heads were better than one.

The fireplace doors rattled with the fury of a trapped animal trying to free itself, causing Kendra to jump and spill half her glass of wine on the hardwood floor. She hurried to her desk and scrambled through a drawer stuffed with odds and ends—old photographs, tangled sewing thread, a rusty screwdriver and scraps of crumpled paper—until she found a roll of adhesive tape. Taking her courage in hand she went back to the fireplace and securely taped the doors shut. She was safe, at least for the moment.

Patty arrived, surveyed the situation without comment and poured herself a glass of wine. "You could build a tunnel out of cushions and pillows from the fireplace to the patio doors," she suggested after a moment, settling down in a chair a good distance away from the fireplace. "Then open the patio doors and let him run outside."

"Squirrels can climb," Kendra pointed out impatiently. "They're *famous* for climbing. And what do I do if he climbs right over the tunnel and escapes in my house?" She shuddered. "Squirrels also bite!"

"We could get a box," Patty offered, "and put it over the fireplace opening, and when he jumps inside we'll close the box and he'll be trapped."

"I don't have a box big enough."

"You could always build a fire."

Kendra's response to that was a disparaging look that spoke louder than words.

Patty shrugged. "I could call Ted and see if he has a gun."

"You wouldn't dare!"

Ted was Patty's on-again, off-again boyfriend, and his solution to every problem was invariably physical. Aside from aesthetic considerations, Kendra positively refused to be a party to cold-blooded murder. Although when the fireplace doors began to bang and rattle again in a brief, nerve-wracking cacophony of desperation, she almost had second thoughts.

"All right, all right!" she snapped at the fireplace. "I'm sorry, okay? If you'd stayed in the trees where you belong, none of us would have this problem now. It's not my fault. I'm doing the best I can."

She ran her hand through her hair one more time and flung herself onto the beanbag chair opposite Patty. "Two hundred thousand dollars," she muttered. "Four bedrooms, three baths, a half-acre lot, and what do I get? Heartaches. Nothing but heartaches."

She glared at Patty. "What do I need four bedrooms for? I can only sleep in one at a time. What do I want with a formal dining room? I don't even have time to eat, much less shop for a dining-room suite. And do you know what lives in beamed ceilings? Spiders, that's what. I never had spiders in my apartment."

Patty gave a negligent lift to her shoulders. "So call an exterminator."

Kendra seized on that. "Exterminator. Do you think they know anything about squirrels?"

"They know how to exterminate them," Patty pointed out, and Kendra let her shoulders sag. If at all possible, she wanted to take the animal alive.

"God," Kendra moaned. "How did I ever let you talk me into this?"

"It was a good investment," Patty replied patiently, just as she had when she had first started her campaign to persuade Kendra to buy the house. "You're twenty-eight years old and still living like a gypsy. No one in your income bracket rents, for heaven's sake. Besides, we need someplace to entertain our clients and impress them with our design skills. You certainly couldn't do that in that tacky little apartment of yours. Of course—" she glanced around at the half-empty, haphazardly furnished room "—not that this is much better, so far."

"You're in my income bracket," Kendra pointed out acerbically. "I don't notice you rushing out to buy a house."

"I sell real estate," Patty answered in a tone that had sounded perfectly reasonable to Kendra when she had first used it two months ago. "I don't buy it. Besides—" she took a sip of her wine "—do you think I want to be saddled with all these problems?"

Kendra only glared at her.

The two women had been friends since Kendra had first moved to Sacramento fresh out of college. Patty had at that time been working for a large real-estate firm, and it was she who helped Kendra find the apartment in which she had lived until two weeks ago. Patty was already on her way to building a respectable name for herself in the real-estate business; Kendra was just beginning her career as an interior designer.

Then Patty made the biggest sale of her life to an Arabian oilman who had only one condition—that the house be completely furnished to his exacting taste and ready to live in by the time the deal closed. Patty had called Kendra.

When Kendra told the story at cocktail parties, it all sounded so easy—a fairy-tale beginning to a spectacular career. It had in fact been the most frightening—and exhilarating—thing she had ever done in her life. The exhilaration was in working with an unlimited budget; the nightmare was in trying to design a dream house, from towels to toilet-seat covers, for an absentee client whose vague suggestions were unhelpful and whose concrete demands were unworkable.

But somehow she had done it, and it worked. It worked so well in fact that the next call Patty got was from an executive who was under the impression that Patty specialized in made-to-order, completely furnished luxury homes. That was where the idea for Dream Houses was born.

From the beginning, neither had had any concept of just what a timely idea Dream Houses was. Sacramento, California, was one of the fastest growing areas of the United States; it had seemed reasonable to them that transferred executives and heads of corporations might form a small market for ready-to-move-into luxury homes. Indeed, that was how it began. Patty made the sale; Kendra designed the interior. Then they were approached to design the residence for a new consulate, and the resulting publicity caused business to boom. Almost before they knew it, they had progressed to the next logical step—designing and building a client's dream house from the ground up. And no longer was their business limited to the obscenely wealthy with a bent for self-indulgence. It had expanded to include a very obvious market: the young professional couple who, having made their success, now only wanted to enjoy it without being bothered with mundane details like picking out furniture and choosing a silver pattern.

Sometimes Kendra wondered uneasily what their phenomenal success said about the values of the modern world, but in fact the truth was obvious. In the goal-oriented, fast-paced society in which they lived, busy people wanted all the rewards with none of the inconveniences of domestic life; a house was not so much a home as a status symbol, and no one wanted to do himself what he could hire someone else to do for him. When a client moved in to his dream house he only had to bring his suitcases. Every need was anticipated, from the welcome mat at the threshold and the cookware in the kitchen to the matching toilet paper in the bathrooms. The cabinets were stocked with grocery staples, and as a special signature touch, Dream Houses catered a welcome-home candlelit dinner for their client's first night in the new home. In a ready-made world, Dream Houses was an idea whose time had most definitely come.

Now Kendra Phillips and Patricia Dorman had a suite of offices in one of the most prestigious buildings in Sacramento, sales representatives in seven states and projects all over the country. They employed two architects, three secretaries, half a dozen full-time shoppers and numerous support personnel. They had been featured in *Fortune* and *Architectural Digest*. And at times Kendra still had difficulty believing in the enormity of their success, much less dealing with it.

She supposed that there was some kind of karmic justice in the fact that she, who had made a career out of making home ownership painless for others, should be afflicted with the seven plagues of Egypt when she herself bought a house. She just didn't know how to cope.

"You know what your trouble is, don't you?" Patty said, topping off her wineglass from the open bottle on the scarred trunk that served as Kendra's coffee table. "You're fighting this thing, you're bringing all this trouble on yourself. Deep down inside you hate the idea of owning a house so much you're inventing excuses to justify it."

"I did not invent the squirrel," Kendra retorted indignantly. "Any more than I invented the handle that came off the faucet and almost flooded the bathroom before the plumber got here or the exploding water heater or the furnace—''

''That was a blown fuse.''

''Which cost me an eighty-three-dollar service charge to find out. Or the broken drain spout on the gutters or the clogged garbage disposal.''

Patty waved a dismissing hand. ''Nickle-and-dime repairs, minor inconveniences. These little things come up when you own a house.''

''Exactly,'' declared Kendra. ''And I just don't have time to deal with them. Besides,'' she added rather grudgingly, ''I don't hate this house. I love it.''

That was the essence of the problem. As much as she would have liked to blame her friend for the entire fiasco, the truth was Kendra had fallen hopelessly in love at first sight with every detail, from the gracious double-paneled stained-glass door and lustrous maple-wood floors to the carved oak mantle over the fireplace. She had imagined the bubble-shaped glass-walled solarium filled with green plants and wicker furniture. She had seen herself pulling back the recessed paneled doors of the library and stepping into a world filled with leather books and serenity or descending the spiral staircase to greet a room filled with congenial guests and the muted strains of chamber music. She had planned to take a gourmet cooking course to do justice to the spacious country kitchen and to create an elegantly landscaped garden that would be the showplace of the neighborhood.

She had lived here two weeks, and weeds were taking over the flower bed, the library was cold and empty and the glass panels of the solarium were splotched with mud from the latest rainstorm. The only inroad she had made toward decorating was to tack sheets over her bedroom windows for privacy; every other window in the house was glaringly bare. The furniture she had brought from her apartment was not only mismatched and overused, but painfully inadequate. The family room in which she and Patty were sitting now was so empty that there was an echo. And perhaps most distressing of all, her faithful old tomcat had been so traumatized by the move that he had been cowering under the bed. The only way Kendra could tempt him out was by placing a can of tuna at the edge of the dust ruffle, but that solution was never permanent. Lately she had begun to wish she had Maurice's temperament. She would have loved to just hide under the bed and refuse to deal with any of it.

"I guess you're like the cobbler whose children never have shoes," Patty commented. "This place certainly is a mess."

Kendra didn't see the connection and was too tired to try. She was hungry, as well, and realized in dismay that she had forgotten to stop by the grocery store. "What about the squirrel?" she demanded.

"I'm thinking."

"Maybe the petting zoo," Kendra suggested hopefully. "If we called them..."

Patty gave her a condescending look. "You can't *call* someone for everything, Kendra."

"Of course you can. This is America."

"Well, if that's the case, why don't you call for pizza? You interrupted my dinner and I'm starved."

"At least you get to *have* dinner. I haven't had time to fix a meal since I moved in here."

"Like you did *before* you moved? You never had a meal in your life that didn't come out of a cardboard container."

Kendra got up and paced to the fireplace, peering cautiously inside. Everything was quiet . . . for the moment. "So who has time to cook? I barely have time to eat."

Patty sighed. "I thought the whole point of buying this house was to give some stability to your life. But you're in bigger chaos now than you ever were. Look at this place." The sweeping gesture she made around the room included the Spartan furniture, the naked windows, the cluttered desk with its stacks of leaning file folders and drawers overflowing with collected odds and ends. "How can you live like this? You've got to get yourself organized."

"How?" demanded Kendra. "And when? I've got grass growing so high my lawn is in danger of being declared a national wildlife preserve. I don't even have time to shop for food, and you want me to shop for drapes? It's April, and I haven't even sent out my Christmas cards yet. My cat is having a nervous breakdown, my house is being invaded by rodents, and I want you to know I'm wearing my last clean skirt because I don't have time to wait around all day for the service man to come hook up my washing machine. Don't talk to me about getting organized."

"What you need," Patty advised soberly, "is a husband."

"No. What I need is a wife."

Kendra looked back into the fireplace and lowered her voice. "Patty, come here. I think he's gone."

Patty came over and cautiously peeled back the tape that held the doors closed. Two parallel sticky scars were left on the formerly spotless glass doors. "You'll never get that off," Patty commented.

"Let the next owners worry about it. I'm selling this place."

"Only a wimp would be driven out of her home by a squirrel."

"You're not going to open the doors are you?"

"It's now or never. I can't stay here all night. If he's crawled back up the chimney, you've got to close the damper before he comes back down again."

"But what if he's only hiding?"

Patty opened the doors.

A tiny fury of grey fur bolted out of the fireplace and into the room. Kendra screamed. Patty stumbled back and tripped over a hassock. The squirrel dashed across the room and skidded off the television set, dislodging a mountain of magazines in the process. A lamp overturned. Patty scrambled toward the patio doors and flung them open. The squirrel leapt for the desk and sent piles of papers and folders flying. Kendra chased the animal across the room, waving her arms and shouting, and the terrified creature dived for the open door, scrambled across the threshold and disappeared into the night.

The aftermath of disaster was still and silent. The two women looked at each other, breathing hard. Then Patty said, "The next time you call me, I'm not going to be home."

Patty closed and locked the patio doors, and Kendra went over to the fireplace. She fumbled inside the chimney for the damper, and a cloudburst of soot descended on her arm as she pulled the handle down.

Kendra stood up, brushing at her ruined and blackened sweater with stunned, ineffective movements.

Patty regarded her with the patient sympathy one might give to a demented child.

"You need to have your chimney cleaned," she advised unnecessarily. "And I—" she swept up her purse and started for the door "—need to find you a husband."

Two

Since moving into the house Kendra had had no need for an alarm clock. At precisely six-forty-five every morning the sun would burst through the gaps between the tacked-up sheet and the window frame, pierce Kendra's eyes and set off a thundering headache. She would wrestle with the inevitable for fifteen minutes, turning, covering her face with the pillow, groaning out loud and muttering curses before finally giving up and staggering out of bed. Mornings had never been her favorite time of day, but things had definitely gone downhill since the mornings had begun to announce themselves in such an obscene way.

At seven o'clock she pulled a short kimono over her teddy and groped her way downstairs to the kitchen. She grimaced at the chaos that greeted her: unwashed coffee cups and cereal bowls, stained counters and scattered coffee grounds, the table covered with half-opened mail. Empty milk cartons, a spilled bag of potato chips and a hammer-and-nails-cluttered butcher block work island. The sink was occupied by the sweater she had tried to soak clean last night, and the country brick floor was dull with the mud she had tracked in from Tuesday's rainstorm.

"Not exactly *Better Homes and Gardens*," she muttered, and promised herself that sometime today she would at least load the dishwasher.

She filled the coffeepot, groped in the cabinet for the package of chocolate cookies she distinctly remembered buying some time within the last two weeks and found there was only one cookie left. It was slightly stale, but she ate it anyway. She was opening a can of tuna for Maurice when the doorbell rang.

That was not a usual thing. Since moving in the only visitor she ever had was Patty, and even Patty had sense enough not to stop by at this hour of the morning. She reached the foyer just as the doorbell chimed again, and all she could make out through the stained-glass panel was the form of a man. *Probably some neighbor come to complain about the height of the grass,* she thought with an inward groan, and opened the door cautiously a few inches.

"Yes?"

The man had indeed been gazing over her lawn, and when he turned, a hint of critical appraisal still remained on his face. But when she spoke that look dissolved into a smile that brought sunshine into his green eyes, and even in her groggy state Kendra couldn't help doing some appraising of her own.

His hair was dark and glinted with a copper hue in the sunlight. His face was bronze and narrow with a faint ridge to the set of his aquiline nose that could have indicated it had been broken at some time. There was a crease in his cheek when he smiled that gave an endearing look to his otherwise harsh features. He was wearing a dark blue blazer, gray slacks and an Oxford shirt, all of which complimented his lean form to such perfection that he could have stepped out of an ad from *Country Gentlemen* magazine. He stood with one hand tucked casually in the pocket of his slacks, regarding her with that lazy, easy smile, and Kendra thought, *Not bad.* If one had to be disturbed at this ungodly hour of the morning by a complaining neighbor, this definitely was the way to do it. Perhaps she would reconsider selling the house.

He said, "Ms. Phillips?" His voice was smooth and rich and very pleasant to the ear. "I'm Michael Drake from Househusbands, Incorporated. I hope I'm not calling too early."

She took the business card he offered her in some confusion and disappointment, glanced at it and tried to hand it back. "I'm sorry, I don't need any—"

"I believe a Miss—" he consulted a small black notebook that he took from his jacket pocket "—Dorman placed the order. Your business partner?"

Kendra stared at him. "Patty?"

"Patricia Dorman, that's right. She asked if I could come over right away."

"Here?"

She didn't seem to be able to do anything but stare at him stupidly and make blank remarks, but he was polite enough to pretend not to notice. He merely smiled and nodded. "That's right."

Kendra looked at the card in her hand, self-consciously clutching her kimono closed at the chest with the other—although from his vantage point at the door he could have had no more than a four-inch-wide glimpse of her under the best of circumstances. She read the lettering on the card three times slowly: Househusbands, Inc. Domestic Management, and in smaller script, Michael Drake. On the third reading she remembered Patty's parting comment about finding her a husband, and the pieces clicked together with a snap of utter incredulity.

She glanced at Mr. Drake, who was still waiting patiently, and then at the card. She said, "Umm—will you excuse me for a moment?" And quickly closed the door.

She hurried to the telephone and first dialed the number on the business card. A pleasant recorded female voice answered. "You have reached the offices of Househusbands, Incorporated. Our business hours are from nine to five Monday through Friday, but if you will—"

Kendra hung up and punched out Patty's number.

"What is this man doing on my front porch?" she demanded when Patty's sleepy voice answered.

"Have you got an easier question?"

"This—this—" Kendra consulted the card again "—this house husband person!"

"Oh, is he there already?" Patty's voice perked up. "That's service, for you."

"You mean you did call him?"

"Of course I did. I told you I would."

"Are you crazy? You can't just look in the phone book and find a husband!"

"Sure you can. This is America, remember?"

Kendra drew in a breath through her teeth, ran her fingers through her hair and turned back to the door.

His figure was still silhouetted against the glass. "All right," she said, deliberately calming her voice. "All right. Let's just start at the beginning, okay? Just because it's seven o'clock in the morning and I'm standing here half naked while a man waits at the door claiming to be my husband and I haven't even had my coffee yet is no reason to get upset, right? I'm sure you can explain everything. So start explaining."

"It's very simple," Patty replied patiently, muffling a yawn. "When I got home last night I remembered this article I'd seen on house husbands—you know, kind of like maids for executive women. So I looked in the telephone book and sure enough, there he was. I got an answering machine but he called me right back and I explained the situation, and—" a note came into her voice that was almost, but not quite, apologetic "—I really didn't think he'd be this fast. I thought I'd tell you about it first."

"Oh, you did, did you? How gracious." Kendra took another sharp breath and tried to think of some reason why she should not be irritated with Patty, but none was forthcoming. She gripped the phone as though it were Patty's neck, and she inquired deliberately, "You gave my address to a perfect stranger over the telephone?"

Patty hesitated. "Not smart, huh?"

Kendra opened her mouth and let it snap shut again. There was no answer to that that would not exceed the bounds of decency and FCC regulations. And after all these years she knew it was pointless to argue with Patty after the fact. The only thing that surprised Kendra at all was *why* she was surprised at what Patty had done.

She took another calming breath, released it slowly, and said quietly into the telephone, "I'll see you at the office, Patty. Goodbye."

She replaced the receiver in the cradle with a distinctly unsatisfactory thump and spent a few more moments glaring at it before turning, reluctantly, to the problem at hand. She looked at the card, and then at the door. She couldn't just leave him standing there, and chances were that he was exactly who the business card said he was—though what, exactly, that was she still wasn't quite sure. Her headache had grown to a dull throb that spread all the way down her neck, and she just wasn't up to dealing with this. She thought again of Maurice cowering under the bed and longed to join him.

Finally, seeing no other choice, she belted her kimono firmly around her waist, made an attempt to smooth down her hair and went back to the door.

"I'm terribly sorry, Mr. Drake," she began, forcing a pleasant smile onto her features, "but it seems there was a misunderstanding—"

"Oh, that's perfectly all right. I should have called first but I didn't know you weren't expecting me. And since I live nearby, I thought we could get this preliminary interview out of the way before you left for work. That will give us the whole day to get started here. May I come in?"

"Well . . ."

But even as he spoke he was moving through the door, and Kendra, momentarily disoriented, moved back to allow him entrance. It might have been her imagination, but it seemed that when she stepped back his eyes lingered for a fraction of a second too long on her legs.

He grasped the door to close it behind him and then paused to examine the handle. "I don't like this lock," he said. "Skeleton key, right? That's the trouble with these antique doors—beautiful, but no security. You need to install a dead bolt."

"Well, I was going to—"

"No problem. We can take care of that for you."

He moved through the foyer, his busy eyes sweeping the surroundings with practiced scrutiny—the spiral staircase, the cut-glass chandelier, the mullioned windows. Kendra trailed behind him, trying to find a polite way to tell him that he had made a mistake and feeling more than a little self-conscious with bare legs and rumpled hair. She had just opened her mouth to speak when he stopped short at the entrance to the family room, and she almost bumped into him.

His eyes moved over the room with slow deliberation, absorbing the toppled lamp, the magazines and papers littering the floor, the tiny soot marks in the shape of squirrel's feet that dotted the white walls, the sagging furniture, the portable television set on its rickety stand and the uncurtained windows smeared with handprints.

He turned his gaze to her, his expression slightly quizzical. "You *are* Kendra Phillips?"

"Yes, but—"

"The designer? From Dream Houses?"

"Well, yes—"

He glanced around the room again, then lifted a quizzical eyebrow. "Redecorating?" he suggested.

Kendra felt color tinge her cheeks, though whether it was from embarrassment or indignation she wasn't quite sure. "Actually, we had a little accident here last night. A squirrel..." His gaze was patient and polite, and she had no intention of going into that story with this self-collected gentleman while standing in her nightgown. "It's not important," she muttered, and avoided his eyes.

He murmured only, "I see."

He crossed the room to pick up a stack of magazines and when he turned back around there was no mistake about it—he was definitely looking at her legs. Under other circumstances there would have been nothing surprising about that at all—in fact, Kendra might have been flattered—but she was at a distinct disadvantage. He was efficient and professional; she was half dressed and disheveled, and the appreciative lingering look he gave her from the toes upward caught her off guard. Kendra felt a schoolgirlish impulse to cross her ankles.

Perhaps the most disconcerting thing was that when his eyes met hers there was nothing in his gaze except polite professionalism—and perhaps a touch of regret. He said, "Ms. Phillips, I'll be frank with you. Our services are rather expensive, and if things are—" his gaze moved around the room again, his reluctance clear "—unsettled in your business at the moment, perhaps now is not the time to—"

Kendra was stung. "I assure you, your fees have nothing to do with anything. Just because things are a mess right now doesn't mean I can't afford—I mean, I don't *live* like this, you know. What I mean to say is..." She struggled for dignity, wondering why in the world she was defending herself and her finances to this man when all she had really intended to do was to get rid of him. "I just moved in, and I'm a little disorganized at the moment, that's all."

His clear green eyes were thoughtful and assessing, and after a moment he nodded. "Well," he said crisply, "let's have a look at the rest of the place, shall we?"

And before she could object, he was moving off. She had no choice but to follow. "Do you live alone?"

"Yes. I mean, no. I have a cat."

"Indoor or outdoor?"

"Under the bed, mostly."

He pulled open the library doors and glanced inside. "Do you bring a lot of work home?"

"Sometimes."

"You'll want to turn this into a study, then."

"Actually, no, I—"

He closed the door and moved down the east hallway. "What time do you get home in the evenings?"

"Seven, eight—it depends." She became alarmed at the personal nature of the questions and quickly asserted herself. "I really don't see what that has to do with anything at all. As I told you before, Mr. Drake, I really don't—"

But he had reached the solarium, and he paused to look inside. "Now this is nice," he said appreciatively. "Automatic sprinklers?"

Kendra blinked. "What?"

"You ought to have an independent water source in here for your plants." He moved along the wall until he found what he was looking for. "Here you go. There are outlets all along the walls that adjust to sprinkle or humidify."

"Oh," said Kendra, somewhat awed. "I didn't know that."

He smiled, and once again his gaze swept across her legs. Kendra's irritation reasserted itself, but just as she was about to speak, he moved past her and started down the hall. He walked with long confident strides that caused Kendra to double her steps in order to keep up, and that fact, perhaps irrationally, only increased her annoyance. No one should move through another person's house with such authority, especially when he was uninvited. He made her feel like a tourist in her own home.

"How many bedrooms?" he tossed over his shoulder.

"Four. But—"

"Baths?"

"Three."

"Outside entrances?"

She did some calculation in her head. "Three—four . . . I don't know." And then she stopped, scowling. "What are you, a burglar or a housekeeper?"

Again he chuckled. "Neither."

But his amusement faded as he reached the kitchen. He merely stood there, hands in pockets, surveying the disaster detail by detail for an embarrassingly long time. Then he released a low breath and said softly, "Well."

And that was enough. If anyone had barged into her office like that, firing off personal questions and quick judgments she would have put him in his place within the blink of an eye. She ran her office with an iron hand; no one intimidated her, no one got past her. In the office she was efficient, businesslike and organized, never flustered, never ruffled. This arrogant, demanding man wouldn't have stood a chance in her office; why was she letting him walk all over her in her own home?

And he had seemed like such a nice person when she first opened the door.

She began firmly, "Mr. Drake—"

He had moved to the counter by the sink, where a battered aluminum pan was soaking out the remnants of a burned can of soup she had prepared three days ago. "You need some new cookware," he commented.

"Well, that may be true, but—"

He lifted the coffeepot and glanced at it critically. "Your coffee maker could use a good cleaning, too. You'd be surprised at the difference it makes in the taste."

Kendra was momentarily speechless.

He picked up the open can of tuna she had left on the counter and turned to her quizzically. "Breakfast?"

"No, cat food. But that's besides the point—"

"Tuna is bad for cats, you know. Causes kidney problems. We feed our pets a mixture of chicken, grains and vegetables—"

"*Your* pets!" Sheer astonishment allowed Kendra to get in the first word at long last, and outrage followed quickly on its heels. This had gone far enough.

Kendra crossed in front of him, squaring her shoulders and placing her hands on her hips. "Mr. Drake," she said sternly, "we've got to get something straight. First of all, what I feed my cat and how I make my coffee is none of your business. Secondly, I don't think all these personal questions you've been asking are in the least appropriate, and I'm not at all sure that I shouldn't be calling the police right now. And thirdly—stop looking at my legs!"

His gaze swept upward with a mild twinkle, and his lips quirked irrepressibly. "Excuse me," he replied. "But it's hard not to."

Then Kendra did cross her ankles, caught herself with a flush, and planted her feet squarely again. She deliberately did not flinch from the amusement in his eyes. "It's also very rude."

"You're right, and I'm sorry." But he didn't look sorry. He looked every bit as domineering as he had from the moment he had sailed through her door. "I'm also sorry if my questions offended you, but they're necessary. If I accept this job, everything about you is my business, from your brand of toothpaste and your sleeping habits to your cat. And there's no need to call the police; we're fully bonded and insured. Now, was there a fourthly?"

Once again Kendra was disoriented by his direct-ness—or perhaps it was the way the morning sunlight played in his forest-green eyes—and she blinked. "What?"

"You were saying . . . ?" he prompted.

"Oh. Yes." She took a breath and restrained the urge to tighten the belt on her kimono, protecting herself from his lazy gaze. "The fact is, this has all been a mistake." She reinforced her words with a cool smile, and was quite proud of her businesslike tone. "My partner never should have called you without asking me first, because if she had consulted with me I could have saved us both some time. I'm afraid I really have no need for your services."

He shook his head and chuckled softly. "Ms. Phil-lips, you have more need for my services than anyone I've ever known. As a matter of fact—" he glanced around the kitchen again "—this will probably be the biggest challenge of my career."

Kendra barely restrained a very unprofessional stomp of her foot. "There isn't going to be any challenge. I'm not employing you!"

"That's your decision, of course. You have my card; we can talk later. Right now—" he glanced at his watch "—you have to be at work in little over an hour, so I suggest you get dressed. I'll let myself out. I want to look over the yard before I go."

"But—"

"Have a nice day, Ms. Phillips."

He left by the back door, leaving Kendra frustrated, speechless and feeling very much like the whole business was far from over. And if there was one thing Kendra hated, it was unfinished business.

The office was a haven for Kendra. The gentle pomegranate-colored carpet, the gray walls with puce accents, the recessed lighting, the subdued clatter of computer keys and the muted purr of telephones—that was her refuge, and there she sought escape from the freneticism of daily living. Everything was in order, everything was predictable, and Kendra was in control.

Her secretary greeted her with a smile and the morning mail, already opened and sorted in order of importance. There were no calls, and Kendra took her monogrammed coffee cup and her mail into her private office and closed the door.

If her home was the reflection of a deranged and cluttered mind, her office was the mirror of her more serene and, Kendra liked to think, truer self. The decor was peach and spring green with generous splashes of white—in the buttersoft leather sofa, the abstract prints on the walls, the enameled legs of her glass-topped desk. The room was almost one-third windows, spilling light over her drawing board and work area. It was fresh, airy and ultimately conducive to the creative side of her personality. Sometimes she thought she would be much happier if she just moved a daybed into the office and took up permanent residence there.

She began the day as she always did, by sinking into a plush peach contour chair, kicking off her shoes and settling back with her coffee and her mail. For half an hour she would immerse herself in the soothing rhythms of the office and endeavor to forget the disastrous way the morning had begun.

But today it was not to be so easy. She had just taken the first sip of her coffee—whose pot, apparently, was cleaned regularly, for it was always delicious—when there was a timid knock at the door. Patty stepped inside.

"I brought a peace offering," she said. She held in her hands an open box of glazed pastries.

Never were the differences between the two partners more apparent than when they were side-by-side in the work environment. Patty, the saleswoman, was the perfect corporate representative with her glimmering blond pageboy, her perfectly tanned skin and conservative business suits. She had a petite, round figure, a warm smile and a firm handshake. Everything about her was designed to instill confidence in a prospective client.

Kendra, on the other hand, was the artist, and her appearance proclaimed the fact. Her dark hair was cropped short, shaved at the neck and full on the top in a high-fashion look. Her milky white skin, high cheek-bones and expressive brown eyes gave her face a touch of gauntness, and her tall small-boned build made her look slender despite the fact that her love for sweets kept her fighting a constant weight problem. Her wardrobe was eclectic, and her unique style was designed for comfort, not public impressions.

Today she was wearing a khaki cotton sundress with a slim dropped bodice and a long full skirt—and that had been found only after a frantic search through the back of her closet for something, anything, that was clean. She had topped it off with an oversize gauze shirt tied low on the waist, a pair of clunky silver earrings and a collection of bangle bracelets. She looked stylish, breezy and casual, but in comparison to Patty in her powder-blue Dior suit and ruffled blouse she felt like the "before" picture of a magazine make-over ad.

She glared at Patty for a moment, feeling as though the other woman's fresher-than-thou appearance were reason enough to hold a grudge without even considering the torment she had endured for Patty's sake that morning. It didn't take long, however, for the lure of the pastries to win out, and reluctantly Kendra surrendered.

"Okay, give," she demanded, and held out her hands for the pastry box.

Patty gave a chuckle and moved into the room. She set the pastries on the glass table beside Kendra, pulled up a chair and settled down eagerly with her own coffee cup. "Well? What happened?"

Kendra selected a cherry Danish and a paper napkin. "Will you let me enjoy my breakfast before I have to end this partnership?"

"Oh, come on, Kendra, I was only trying to help. What's wrong with that?"

Kendra took one bite out of her Danish, fixed Patty with a steely gaze and swallowed at leisure before she answered. "You wouldn't have to ask that if you'd had your home invaded by an efficiency expert at seven o'clock in the morning, who marched around like a drill sergeant snapping questions and looking for a spit-shine on the Tupperware, for heaven's sake!" Kendra's indignation rose as she recalled the episode. "Do you know he even had the gall to ask if I could *afford* his services?"

Patty choked on laughter and quickly held her coffee cup away from her body to avoid spilling on the spotless suit. "Well, Kendra, you've got to admit your life-style is not exactly of the rich and famous. You can't blame the guy for being a little confused. So, what did you tell him?"

Kendra took another vicious bite out of her pastry. "What do you think I told him? I told him to get lost, that's what."

Patty sighed. "I was afraid of that."

"Well, what did you expect?"

"A little common sense, perhaps?" Patty took a bear claw from the box and spread a napkin carefully over her crossed knees. She looked at Kendra earnestly. "Listen, kid, you're my friend and I love you, but you have got to get your act together. I can't keep running over to your place every time something breaks down, and God knows how long you'll be able to live in that mess before it's condemned by the board of health . . . so what's wrong with having a housekeeper? You need a housekeeper. You need *something*."

Kendra took another bite of her pastry, uncomfortably considering the truth behind Patty's words. "So why can't I have a female housekeeper?"

"What has sex got to do with anything?" Patty demanded in exasperation, and then added more patiently, "I'll tell you why you can't have a female housekeeper. Because of the time you tried to light a fire with the damper closed or the time you broke the handle off the faucet and couldn't find the water shut-off valve, and the time you tried to replace a switch-plate and almost electrocuted yourself. Because men *know* things, that's why. And these guys also do handy work."

Kendra paused with the Danish halfway to her mouth, her attention caught. "He *did* say something about replacing the lock on my front door," she murmured.

"See?" Patty insisted triumphantly. "There are a dozen pesky little chores this person could take off your hands. You're an *executive*, Kendra, a busy executive, you don't have time to waste taking out garbage and mowing the lawn. You need a man around the house."

Kendra gave Patty a wry look as she finished off the cherry Danish. "You're a busy executive, too. I don't notice you rushing out to hire a house husband."

"I don't have to," Patty replied smugly. "I've got Ted."

"Ha!" Kendra reached for a cheese Danish. "Until the next time you break up again."

Patty shrugged. "So the next time I need something done around the place I'll make up with him. That's what men are good for, after all, and they just love a helpless woman."

Kendra chewed thoughtfully. "It would be kind of nice, I guess, to have somebody take care of the house. Maybe do a little gardening, patch that hole under the sink . . ."

"Change the light bulb in the garage," Patty suggested.

"Maybe hang some drapes and help move the furniture when the carpet comes . . ." Kendra was warming to the subject. "Clean the oven and unstick that window that's painted shut . . ."

But then her face fell. "But not Michael Drake. He was impossible. We didn't get along at all."

"You don't have to *marry* the man," Patty replied impatiently. "Just let him clean your house. Besides," she pointed out, "this was an agency. If you don't like the fellow they sent over this morning, ask for someone else."

Kendra hesitated, greatly tempted. When Patty explained it, it sounded like the perfect solution . . . but then all of Patty's ideas sounded perfect until they were put into practice. Like buying the house, for instance.

Kendra shook her head. "I don't know. The whole thing just makes me uneasy. All those personal questions—what time do I get home, how many doors and windows do I have, what do I feed my cat, for heaven's sake. He could have been casing the joint, for all I know. How do I even know he was who he said he was?"

"Call the agency," Patty advised, "and find out."

That was one idea that only improved upon examination. The more Kendra thought about it, the more uncomfortable she became with the memory of Michael Drake striding through her house, examining every nook and cranny, lock and window. After a moment she put down the Danish and scrambled through her purse for the business card he had left her. She punched out the number.

"Househusbands, Incorporated. May I help you?"

Kendra raised an eyebrow at Patty. At least she had gotten a real person this time instead of a recording. "Umm, yes. I'd like to check the references of one of your employees."

The voice on the other end might have held a faint note of surprise. "Yes ma'am?"

"Michael Drake."

Now there was no mistaking the surprise in the silence that followed, and there was a hint of frostiness in the secretary's tone. "Mr. Drake is not an employee."

Kendra cast a triumphant look toward Patty. Patty quickly stretched across the desk and pressed the speaker button, and the secretary's next words were broadcast over the room. "Mr. Drake is the owner."

Now it was Kendra's turn for a surprised silence and Patty's turn for triumph. Before Kendra could reply, Patty spoke up, "Would you connect me, please?"

"One moment, please."

Kendra hissed, "What did you do that for?"

Patty gave her a kind, faintly condescending smile. "Do you remember when we first started this business?"

"Of course."

"And who did we decide would deal with the public?"

Kendra was beginning to see her point. "You. But—"

"Do you remember why we decided that?"

"Because I don't do it very well," she admitted grudgingly. "But—"

"So if I know you, and I do, you owe Mr. Drake an apology at the very least."

A male voice came through the speakerphone. "Michael Drake."

Kendra winced, stared at the phone and cleared her throat. "Mr. Drake," she said pleasantly. "This is Kendra Phillips."

"Oh, yes. The lady who has no need of my services." There was amusement in his tone. "Having second thoughts?"

Kendra picked up a pen and began to doodle nervously on the scratch pad at her elbow. "Actually, I was afraid I might have been a little rude to you this morning."

"Were you? I didn't notice."

Patty elbowed Kendra hard in the arm, giving her a meaningful look. Kendra scowled at her, but found herself saying, "And I was thinking—maybe I was a little hasty. If I could have a little more information about your agency's services . . ."

"Fine." There was a brief pause. "I can get free here about eleven-thirty. Shall we meet for lunch?"

"Well, actually . . ." Kendra never went out for lunch, and eleven-thirty was far too early.

"Do you know the International Café on Walnut Street?"

"Yes, but—" She definitely didn't want to have lunch with him.

"Good. I'll meet you there." The line was disconnected.

Kendra slowly punched the button on the phone and turned a dour look on Patty. "Looks like we're having lunch," she said.

Patty smiled smugly and settled back to enjoy her pastry.

Three

The April day was bright and warm, and the lunch-time rush was in full force. Kendra remembered why she had made it a policy never to go out at lunch: when Kendra worked, she immersed herself completely, and with the distraction of all this color and bustle it would take her hours to get back into the flow.

Several times during the morning she had almost called Michael Drake to cancel, but with all the vacillation between calling and not calling she hadn't been able to concentrate on her work anyway, and she finally decided that, having wasted the whole morning, another hour at lunch wouldn't kill her. Besides, by now she was curious, and Patty's idea grew in appeal the longer it lingered.

If only she could find someone to straighten up the house now and then, make a few minor repairs, take care of the lawn, how much simpler her life would be.

So much pressure would be taken off her if she didn't have to worry about all those minor inconveniences of home ownership. And this time she wouldn't let Michael Drake intimidate her. He had caught her off guard this morning, but now she was in control. She would be conducting the interview, not he, and matters were certain to go more smoothly now that her legs were decently covered.

The International Café was a sprawling structure that offered an international buffet and a more traditional dining menu, with both indoor and outdoor seating. It was busy and noisy and not the sort of place Kendra would have chosen for a business meeting. However, the dessert bar was famous all over the state, and she was looking forward to indulging her sweet tooth, if nothing else.

Michael Drake met her at the entrance. "Ms. Phillips, right on time I see." He took her hand in a firm businesslike shake. "I've reserved a table for us on the patio."

"Thank you, but I'd prefer to sit inside." She liked the grip of his hand—strong, warm and brief. She had always prided herself on her ability to judge a man's character by the quality of his handshake, and she judged Michael Drake to be solid, forthright and competent. That was a good start.

But the positive tone of the meeting began to slide immediately downhill when he merely glanced at her critically and replied, "Nonsense. You could use the sun." He took her arm in a light grip and began to lead her around the side of the building. "You don't get outdoors much, do you?"

"No, and I don't like the sun. That's why I'd rather sit inside."

"An hour or so won't hurt you. Take advantage of the vitamin D."

Kendra considered arguing with him, but decided it wasn't worth making a scene. And besides, she wasn't at all certain she would win. So she merely pulled out a pair of dark glasses and accepted the chair he pulled out for her at a table on the edge of the patio overlooking a park filled with brilliant red-and-orange tulip beds. The April sunlight, muted by the dark glasses, was warm and soothing, and the view was magnificent. She grudgingly admitted to herself that dining outside might not be such a bad idea after all.

The waitress was prompt with the menus. "Would you like a drink before you order?" she inquired.

Having lunch out was a treat for Kendra, and she thought she might as well go all the way. She was just about to order a champagne cocktail when Michael spoke up.

"Iced tea for both of us will be fine," he said. "And we'll order now, too."

He must have seen Kendra's look of objection, because he added with an inquiring tilt of his head, "You don't drink during business hours, do you?"

"No, of course not," Kendra mumbled uncomfortably, and buried herself in the menu.

Michael ordered a shrimp salad, and though Kendra would have preferred to partake of the more exotic buffet, she could see he was in a hurry. It would probably be best to get this meeting over with as soon as possible, anyway. She ordered a cheeseburger and fries and, as a defiant afterthought, a chocolate milk shake.

Michael wasted no time. He reached into his pocket for the small black notebook and said, "Now, I have just a few more questions for you, Ms. Phillips—"

"If you don't mind, Mr. Drake," Kendra interrupted firmly, "I'd like to ask the questions this time." She was pleased with the decisive tone in her voice. He might be able to bulldoze her aside in the domestic department, but she was on her own turf now. In the world of business she was a dynamo, and the sooner he found that out the better.

He leaned back and smiled. "Of course." When he smiled it was difficult to remember what a domineering person he was, and Kendra almost relaxed. He was not wearing sunglasses, and the light reflected in his eyes was like the play of sun on water. The breeze ruffled his casually cut hair slightly, highlighting the intriguing color with fiery tones. She had never seen hair quite that shade before—jet black with tips of red.

He was waiting, and Kendra realized that, having gained control of the conversation, she wasn't really sure what to do with it. She cleared her throat, folded her hands in her lap and said, "Well, to begin with— I'm not exactly sure what a house husband is. I mean, what do you do, precisely?"

"We do," he answered, "everything a wife would do." And then he grinned. "Except one thing. We haven't figured out how to give birth yet."

She was somewhat disconcerted. "What a pity," she murmured. "I don't suppose you could be more specific?"

"We clean your house, cook your meals, run errands, make minor repairs, do yard work, shop, plan and supervise parties and act as personal secretaries when necessary. We can take over your home accounting, manage your budget, provide emergency transportation, housesit when you travel and, when specialized services are called for—like major home repairs, travel arrangements, et cetera—we deal with the middlemen. All you have to do is sign the checks.''

The rapidity with which he rattled off the list momentarily took Kendra's breath away. "My goodness,'' she managed after a moment. "And all I wanted was someone to mow my lawn.''

He smiled. "You need a great deal more than that, and we're here to provide it. We cater to the executive woman who doesn't have the time or, frankly, the skill, to deal with the mundanities of running a home. Just imagine the perfect husband. That's exactly what we try to be.''

The iced tea arrived then, and Kendra was grateful to take a long cooling sip. She imagined Michael Drake as the perfect husband, and it was both appallingly easy and painfully difficult to do. The strong lean arms, the bronzed skin, the sparkling eyes, the intriguing crease in his cheek...that part was easy. But living with him...

She said, as diplomatically as possible, "You don't—er—live in?''

He shook his head firmly. "Strictly against policy. But we are on call twenty-four hours a day. We realize that household emergencies are not limited to business hours, and we're here to take care of all your needs.''

All her needs. Now, that definitely had possibilities. Perhaps it was the sun or the unexpected festivity associated with going out to lunch, but Kendra found herself looking at Michael Drake in a whole new light. His shirt was unbuttoned at the collar, and the sunlight glinted on a sprinkling of dark hair at his throat. His hands were long and bronzed, and he wore no wedding ring. He had an air of casual elegance and understated strength about him as he lounged across from her, completely at ease with himself and what he had to offer, and those were qualities any woman would find attractive. It was too bad he was such an insufferable boor.

His lips quirked at one corner as he effortlessly read her mind. "All your *household* needs," he clarified, and a glint of amusement sparked briefly in his eyes as Kendra shifted her weight uncomfortably and took another quick sip of her tea.

"We don't encourage our clients to associate with the employees socially," he went on seriously. "We realize that there are going to be times when you need a date for a banquet or a wedding or an awards dinner, and it would be all too easy to ask one of our guys to step in. But there are escort services for that sort of thing, and the client has to realize that if an employee accepts a social invitation he does so at the risk of his job."

Kendra couldn't help being impressed by his thoroughness, by the utter seriousness with which he regarded what was, after all, a rather bizarre occupation. She murmured, "You do think of everything, don't you?"

He smiled. "A lot of our clients are wealthy, single women. The temptation is there—on both parts. We have to protect the reputation of the agency."

"Are all your clients women?"

"Not at all. Many are couples whose professions preclude a normal family life and whose needs aren't met by an ordinary housekeeper. Some of our clients are men who—just like you—don't have time for domestic details. And some are families with children. And not all our clients are wealthy—some are single women with kids who just need someone on call for repairs and maintenance and occasional babysitting. We have a package designed for every situation."

Kendra was intrigued. "And these employees of yours . . . who are they?" What she really meant was, "What kind of man would want to do this type of work?" and he understood.

"Some are college students, some are retirees, but a surprising number work full-time. Misplaced husbands, you might say, who've found that the thing that gives them the most satisfaction out of life is working around the house. You'd be amazed how deep that domestic instinct runs in most men—maintaining a home, improving things, taking care of children—especially when they're using it as a substitute for their own family or the family they never had. Do you know how many men use their vacation time to just tinker around the house? It's the same sort of thing." And he grinned. "Of course, it helps that they get to leave their happy little families at the end of the day, and they get paid very well."

"Fascinating," Kendra murmured. And then she shook her head. "And weird."

"Not really. It's just an example of targeting the market and fulfilling the need."

She shrugged uncomfortably. "It just seems like—such an eighties thing to do."

"Very much like your business," he pointed out. "We live in a service-oriented society. No one wants to do anything for themselves anymore. They're too intent on the immediate reward, goal achievement, getting ahead, making a profit. No one is interested in taking the time to build the foundation anymore—so they buy ready-make houses and ready-made homes."

Kendra wasn't sure she liked the comparison—between her own business and his, and between herself and his self-centered, high-powered client list. But she certainly did not want to examine the differences too closely, not at this point.

What she really wanted to know was why *he* had chosen such a line of work, but she didn't feel comfortable asking that, either. She said instead, trying not to be too blatant about it, "I don't suppose you actually do the jobs yourself, being owner of the company and all."

"I meet the clients and do the initial assessment personally," he answered, "then I generally assign someone. I don't usually go out in the field, so to speak."

Kendra relaxed. An ingenuous college boy or a comfortable old man she might be able to deal with, but Michael Drake...

"Yours is a specialized case, though," he went on, "and I think I'd better take it on myself. However, what I would like to do is bring in a team this afternoon just to get a head start on the place."

Kendra's eyebrows flew up, and she had to take a quick gulp of tea to drown an indignant retort. A team!

Fortunately for Michael Drake—or perhaps for Kendra—the food arrived just then, and it was several moments before she was required to make a reply. By that time she had a grip on her injured dignity, and she was able to keep her tone polite but firm.

"I don't think that will be necessary, Mr. Drake. You see, I'm not sure I'd be at all comfortable with a man around my house, and . . ."

His understanding nod spared her the necessity of finishing. "That's perfectly all right. A lot of people feel that way." She relaxed until he continued, "You never have to see me. I won't arrive until after you leave in the morning, and I'll be gone before you get home."

Kendra gave in to exasperation and concentrated on her hamburger.

For a while they ate in silence, and then he inquired, "How did you get started in Dream Houses, Ms. Phillips?"

Kendra told him her usual cocktail party story about the origins of the business, relaxing in his easy interest until she realized that he must know most of the story already—they had received a lot of publicity recently, after all—and his attentiveness must be feigned. Still, he was good at pretending, and it was enlightening to learn he could be a pleasant luncheon companion when he wasn't being overbearing and commanding.

"So anyway," Kendra finished with a shrug, lifting her milk shake, "we thought it would be just a sideline, something to do in our spare time. Neither Patty nor I ever expected it to take off like it did, a real overnight success, and I'm still not sure I believe it."

His smile was understanding and invited confidence. "So," he inquired easily, leaning back in his chair, "how did you let your life get into such a mess?"

"It's not a mess," Kendra defended, but his patient, nonjudgmental gaze made her feel childish.

There was no point in denying what he had already seen for himself to be the truth.

After a moment she shrugged and sipped her milk shake through the straw. "I don't know," she admitted. "For the last few years I've been working so hard...doing nothing but work, hardly coming up for air. And then all of a sudden—success. Tax advisors, accountants, investment counselors...I mean, I just never saw it coming, you know?" She had a puzzled frown on her face as she tried once more to grapple with the consequences of having "made it," and then sighed.

"I know, I'm a partner in a major corporation and still living like a college student." She focused her attention on the swirls she was making in her milk shake. "Most of my furniture came from my parent's attic. I haven't had a new set of sheets or towels in ten years. But those things don't really interest me, you know?" She looked at him. "Doing it for other people is one thing, but doing it for myself seems redundant."

She dipped her straw into the milk shake a couple of times, then took a sip. "I don't know. I guess the truth is I'm not very comfortable having money, owning a house.... I'm not comfortable with *possessions*. I suppose the only place I am really comfortable is with my work."

He nodded soberly. "That's exactly why you need someone like me. You're an artist, and artists usually don't deal well in the real world. You need a buffer between yourself and all those banal little details that distract you, and my job is to free you to be your creative best."

How wonderful that sounded. His voice was rich and sincere, his expression concerned and involved.

He made her believe, or want to believe, that he would take care of everything. That all she had to do was nod her head and he would make all her problems disappear. It sounded like heaven.

She had to forcefully remind herself that nothing was that easy.

Kendra gave a wry smile and lifted one of her French fries. "I think another thing I'm not comfortable with is letting other people take care of me. I've always been pretty independent."

He inclined his head with a dry lift to his eyebrow. "And you're doing a fine job."

"All right," she admitted, and bit down on the French fry. "So things have gotten a little out of hand lately. But all I need is a little help to get myself organized." She hesitated and looked at him speculatively. "Do you really run errands?"

"Of course."

"Like going to the dry cleaners and the post office and the shoe repair shop?"

"And taking the car in for servicing and standing in line to pay the ad valorem tax—whatever you need."

"And all I'd have to do is leave you a grocery list and you'd do the shopping?"

"You won't even have to leave a list. I'll plan all the menus and leave your meals prepared."

It was like a snowball. The more he said, the more her imagination expanded, and the greater the temptation grew. "And if I had, say, the washing machine man coming, you could wait for him?"

"If I couldn't fix it myself, I'd not only wait for him, but I'd call and make the appointment and write the check when he was finished."

Kendra couldn't help thinking about how much simpler her life would have been if, when the fuse blew or the garbage disposal clogged up, she had had someone like him around to take care of it. Thinking about it almost made her dizzy.

She said, trying hard to keep her tone casual, "And if I had a minor emergency like a car that wouldn't start or, say, a squirrel in the fireplace—I could just call you?"

"And if I couldn't fix it, I'd find someone who could."

She could feel excitement pounding like a pulse in her throat. The possibilities were endless. "And—not that I ever would, of course—but suppose I needed, well, draperies or something. You'd shop for them, have them delivered and get them hung?"

"Ms. Phillips," he said simply. "I would take care of *everything*. All you would have to do is enjoy your work and make the most of your leisure time."

Too good to be true, a far away voice warned her, but Kendra chose not to listen to it. This was surely every woman's fantasy. A tall, strong good-looking man, slave to her every whim, waiting at her beck and call, existing only to serve her. There was probably something a little perverted about that, but also undeniably delightful. *Imagine your dream husband,* he had said, and wasn't this it? A man who had everything under control, who was always there, whose only concern was her well-being. And who, on top of all that, also did windows.

Oh, she knew it was too good to be true, and what had happened to the determined young woman who had practically ordered him out of her kitchen this morning and who had told him less than an hour ago that all she needed was someone to mow her lawn? But, God help her, she was weak, and the temptation was strong. *I'll take care of everything,* he had said.

She heard herself saying in a dazed, airy voice, "Where do I sign?"

He smiled and reached into his pocket, bringing out a sheaf of papers. "I'm glad you brought that up." He opened the document and placed it before her. "We operate on a contractual basis, with a three-month trial period and an option to renew for a year. Our fee is listed at the bottom of page one, payable each month in advance."

Kendra looked at the figure and drew in her breath. "Wow." Her voice sounded a little weak. "You weren't kidding when you said expensive."

"In addition," he warned her, "we have what is called a 'discretionary budget.' This will include miscellaneous household purchases and groceries, for which you'll receive an itemized statement at the end of every month. It makes bookkeeping much simpler."

Kendra shook her head slowly. "It would be cheaper to just get married, wouldn't it?"

He chuckled. "True. If a divorce attorney ever got hold of this, alimony would go through the roof. But then again—" his eyes twinkled "—marriage has certain inconveniences that are eliminated by this contract."

She met his gaze, her own lips twitching with repressed mirth. "Such as?"

"Fighting over the blankets."

Kendra gave in to the smile, but quickly lowered her gaze to the contract again. His eyes, when he was smiling, were very intriguing—and very tempting. Looking at them made her heart beat faster.

She said, trying to keep her voice businesslike, "What if I'm not satisfied or change my mind?"

"Oh, you'll be satisfied," he assured her, and something about his smooth musical voice made her glance up quickly to see whether or not he was still talking about business. He was. "You can cancel anytime within the first three months with a full refund. After that, there's a substantial termination fee."

"I see," she murmured, looking back at the contract. She scanned it rather than read it, for she still hadn't convinced herself that she was really going to sign. She had never done—or even considered doing—anything this crazy in her life.

"Now," he said, pushing aside his plate and turning to his notebook again. "Do you mind if I ask you a few questions?"

"No, of course not," she answered distractedly. She was still thinking about how sexy his eyes looked when he smiled and wondering if she had completely lost her mind. The sun was hot—or maybe it was her racing imagination—and she untied her overshirt and slipped it off her shoulders.

"Do you work weekends?"

"Saturdays, mostly."

"You should take two days off. It will help you rejuvenate, and you'll be more productive." He made a notation in the notebook and glanced up. "I'd keep the shirt on if I were you," he advised. "You're not used to the sun, and you're going to burn."

Deliberately she arranged her shirt over the back of her chair, irritation reminding her that, no matter how

sexy his eyes were, he was not her type. "You're aw-
fully bossy, aren't you?"

"That's my job," he replied easily. "Do you do a lot
of entertaining?"

She gave a dry laugh. "Are you kidding? In that
dump?"

"We can fix that. When are you planning to redecorate?"

"As soon as I get a chance."

"I think we should make arrangements for that
right away." He made another note. "Do you have a
boyfriend?"

That caught her off guard. "No. Why?"

His expression was mild and unabashed. "Purely
professional interest. In case I have to be prepared for
unexpected guests—for dinner, of course."

"Of course." Once again she was irritated, and absently she rubbed the back of her neck where the sun
was, indeed, beginning to burn. "Well, the answer is
no."

"Why not?"

She stared at him, and he grinned unexpectedly.
"*That* was purely personal interest. And you don't
have to answer. Tell me about your cat."

"Maurice?" His changes of mood and his rapid-fire
questions left her feeling disoriented and confused, as
though she were swimming against the tide. "Well,
he's a calico tom who's having a nervous breakdown."

Michael nodded sympathetically. "Probably the
move. Did you try putting butter on his paws?"

"What?"

He made another note. "I'll take care of it."

"I don't want you putting butter on my cat's paws!"

"Do you have any medical problems or dietary requirements I should be aware of?"

"No," she responded, somewhat grumpily. Then, "Can you really cook?"

"I certainly can. Do you jog?"

"No. Why? Do I have to pass a fitness test, too?"

"No." And he glanced at her, that irrepressible twinkle appearing in his eyes. "I just wondered how you got such great legs."

The unexpected compliment tingled in her stomach, and she didn't know how to respond. So she said simply, "Oh."

And then he spoiled it all by adding, "You really should get into some kind of regular exercise program, though. That's an important factor in preventing stress burnout."

The man was growing more irritating by the moment, and Kendra had a sneaking suspicion that he was doing it on purpose—and enjoying it. She scowled. "Do you have a homily for everything?"

He was completely unfazed. "Hazards of the profession, I suppose. Now—" he looked up from his notebook "—we can do this two ways. I can consult with you every morning or every night, whichever is most convenient, and we can discuss the details of what needs to be done and what has already been done; long-term goals and short-term goals—sort of like a board meeting."

Kendra groaned inwardly. If there was one thing she hated more than being bossed around, it was board meetings.

"Or," he went on, "you can leave the decisions completely to me, and I won't bother you until something major comes up."

Plan B had the most appeal from a peace-of-mind standpoint, but there was more than a little uneasiness attached to the concept of allowing him to make all the decisions. In fact, the entire concept was beginning to make her uneasy. It had sounded wonderful when it was only an idea, vague promises of a fantasy life, but now that it was all down in black-and-white on an iron-clad contract, she was having distinct second thoughts—like getting cold feet before the marriage ceremony.

"Well?" he prompted. His expression was patient, his eyes gentle. Then why did she feel as though she was about to jump into a snake pit?

"If we're going to do this thing," she replied reluctantly, "I suppose we may as well go all the way. You make the decisions."

"I agree," he said briskly. "The less you have to worry about the better. And before I forget—" he took another business card from his pocket, and scrawled something on the back "—here's my home phone number. Keep it where you can find it. You can always reach me through the office, but it sometimes takes a while, and there might be an emergency."

"I would never call you at home," she protested.

"Take another look at the figures on the bottom of the page," he advised. "For that amount of money, you deserve twenty-four-hour service. Any time, day or night."

Kendra accepted the card, but assured herself she would never use it.

He offered her his pen. "If you're ready to sign the contract, we can get started today."

She lifted an eyebrow. "No one ever accused you of using the soft sell, I'll bet."

For once he had the grace to look abashed. "I'm sorry. Take all the time you need, of course. You might want to have your lawyers look over the contract."

That was all she needed: one more thing to do, one more pesky detail nagging at the back of her mind. No, she didn't want her lawyers to look over the contract. No, she didn't want to think about it. If she was going to do it, she wanted to get it over with—or not do it at all.

She hesitated, then accepted the pen. "It just seems so—permanent."

A knowing curve softened his smile. "Afraid of commitment?"

"Isn't everyone?"

"In one way or another, I suppose."

She looked up at him. She wondered if he had ever been married. She wondered if he was afraid of commitment and if that was why he took care of other people's families instead of his own. She wondered why she was wasting time speculating about things that were none of her business and that she really didn't want to know.

She glanced back down at the contract.

"Would you like anything else?" the waitress said.

Kendra seized on the reprieve. "Yes, I—"

"Just the check, please," Michael said at the same time, and Kendra glared at him. "We should go," he pointed out. "We've both got work to do, and your shoulders are beginning to burn."

The waitress disappeared, and Kendra said, "I wanted dessert."

A shadow of disapproval crossed Michael's eyes. "I'm going to have to watch your weight, I see."

Kendra's nostrils flared with a sharp breath, and she put the pen down deliberately. "Mr. Drake," she said.

"You can call me Michael."

"Mr. Drake," she repeated distinctly. "There's one thing we'd better get clear right now. I'm twenty-eight years old and I don't need a babysitter. My weight, my health, my sleeping patterns, what I do with my weekends—none of that is your concern. All I need is someone to keep my house and take care of my lawn. I don't need a father, doctor or confessor. So please confine your concern to domestic duties and leave my personal life alone."

He merely smiled. "What you need," he corrected, "is a husband. The word means one who shelters, and nourishes, manages. That's exactly what I'm here to do."

Kendra didn't like the sound of that at all. "No one has ever 'managed' me," she snapped.

He released a soft breath and opened his palms in a gesture of conciliation. "Ms. Phillips," he said, "I'm not trying to make your life more difficult. I'm trying to make it easier. It's not my job to interfere, merely to simplify. I know it's going to take some getting used to, but I think if you'll give me a chance you'll be happier than you've ever been in you life. That's all I want."

The seduction, Kendra thought. How like an earnest lover he sounded, and how many maidens had fallen for that same kind of speech throughout the centuries? *Let me take you away from all this. Come*

live with me and be my love. Let me take care of you.
And she was no more immune to the promise of
happily-ever-after than any woman who had lived before her.

With one important difference, of course. She
wasn't marrying the man. She was only hiring him.
And if he thought for one moment he could manage
her, her life or her cat, he was in for a big surprise.

The waitress brought the check, and Kendra reached
for it. Michael was faster. "Business expense," he
smiled, and took out his wallet.

He placed some bills on the small tray, and Kendra
took up the pen again and drummed it absently
against the contract. It was now or never. She wasn't
going to be haunted by vacillation for the rest of the
week, the rest of the day or even another hour. She
was lured by the glorious vision of a clean house, a
trim lawn, a home-cooked meal waiting when she got
come. She could handle Michael Drake. Why couldn't
she?

But when she put pen to paper she knew exactly how
Faust felt the moment he signed over his soul.

Michael accepted the signed contract with a smile
and tucked it into his pocket. "You won't regret it,"
he promised as he came around to slide out her chair.
"We'll get started this afternoon."

"I think I'm regretting it already," she muttered.

He chuckled softly and put his hand lightly on her
back to escort her out. "Kendra Phillips," he said,
"I'm going to make a new woman out of you."

That was exactly what she was afraid of.

Four

Kendra spent the remainder of the afternoon alternately congratulating herself for the major step she'd made toward reorganizing her life and bemoaning the dreadful mistake she'd made. The day was a complete loss as far as work was concerned. Nonetheless she delayed leaving the office until seven-thirty, half dreading what she would find when she got home.

The first thing she noticed when she stepped into the foyer was a peculiar, faintly familiar scent. Gradually it came back to her from the long-ago days of childhood. "Lemon wax!" she said, and looked around.

The terra-cotta tile of the foyer was scrubbed and shining, the chandelier sparkled, the curving banister gleamed with fresh polish. Even the panes of the twin mullioned windows gleamed.

"All *right*," she declared in soft satisfaction, and moved into the family room.

What she saw there almost made her panic. Everything was so *neat*. The sooty paw prints were scrubbed from the wall, the hardwood floors were buffed to a soft shine, the fireplace doors were polished. Even the wood on her furniture—what little of it there was—gleamed with the effects of hand rubbing. But it was the sight of her desk that caused her heart to leap to her throat.

She flew across the room with a gasp of dismay. The top of her desk was almost completely empty. The drawers were neatly closed—she had never been able to close them before, they were so cluttered with junk. What had he done with her papers? She would never be able to find anything again.

Then she examined the effects of his handiwork more carefully. A slow uncertain relief spread through her. On the top of her desk was an accordion file labeled Household Accounts. Everything appeared to have been neatly filed inside it. Next to the file was a stack of papers bound with a rubber band and labeled Unpaid Bills. When she flipped through it she discovered that each bill was accompanied by a check, completely filled out and awaiting her signature. Apparently he had found her personal checkbook in a desk drawer. That was okay. She had signed over her life to the man, she might as well trust him with her checkbook.

In the center of her desk was a stack of income tax forms, accompanied by another note in his big black handwriting that read, "Why haven't these been filed yet?" She ignored that. She would ask her accountant to file for an extension. She always did.

Cautiously Kendra went into the kitchen, feeling a little like Alice in Wonderland not knowing what surprise awaited her around every corner. She turned on the light.

The floor was waxed, the counters sparkled. Everything was put away, and even the coffeepot gleamed. On the refrigerator was pinned another note: "Dinner is in the refrigerator. Microwave for four minutes."

She looked inside the refrigerator and found not only milk, eggs, yogurt and a quantity of fresh fruit, but a small salad and a plate covered with plastic wrap that contained a serving of chicken in some kind of sauce, asparagus and buttered new potatoes. "Real food!" she exclaimed. She didn't much care for asparagus, and heaven only knew what he expected her to do with all that yogurt, but it *was* real food.

On the top shelf of the refrigerator was a plain white container labeled Cat Food. She opened it and grimaced at the unappetizing concoction she found inside, but a glance at the nearly-empty cat food dish testified to two more miracles: Maurice had apparently left his hiding place some time during the day for the wilds of the kitchen and he had actually eaten Michael Drake's version of a healthy cat diet.

With rising excitement, she began to open cabinet doors. He had stocked her shelves with a variety of canned goods and staples, the paper-towel holder was full, the cleaning supplies arranged neatly under the sink. She didn't see any cookies.

She hurried upstairs and found every bathroom scrubbed within an inch of its life, the floors waxed, the windows cleaned. No wonder he had wanted to bring a team—no single person could have accomplished all this in one afternoon.

Her bed had been made—something she could not recall doing since she moved into the house—her dressing table polished and her toiletries arranged neatly upon it. And most wondrous of all, he had replaced the sheet over the window with a well-fitting window shade. She would sleep tomorrow morning.

Maurice sat at the edge of the dust ruffle and greeted her with a plaintive meow. She laughed in sheer delight and scooped him up. "Well, old boy," she declared, burying her face in the soft fur. "This is what I call living!"

After a moment she went over to her closet and opened the doors. What she saw there almost brought tears to her eyes.

Her clothes were arranged inside, clean, fresh smelling and ironed. He had fixed her washing machine. And done her laundry.

"Oh…my goodness," she said softly. "I think I'm in love."

The dinner was delicious—though it could have used a dessert—and when Kendra slipped between the clean sheets and closed her eyes, Maurice crept up and slept in the crook of her arm for the first time in two weeks. It had only been one afternoon, but already she was happier than she had been in a long, long time.

"Do you know what would be great about having a husband?" Patty said wistfully almost a week later. "Times like this. This stupid speech I have to make to the Realtors' Association at the end of the month. If I had a husband he would pat my hand and say, 'Now, Patty, honey, you don't have to do it if you don't want to. I'll just call the president of the association and tell him you can't make it. Don't you worry your pretty head about it another minute.' And failing that, he'd at least be there to give moral support.''

Kendra glanced up from her drawing board and grinned. ''Better you than me,'' was all the sympathy she had to offer. Patty hated these occasional public appearances because they were stiff and boring, but she was always a hit. Kendra, on the other hand, was terrified of public speaking and could not have been induced at gunpoint to stand up before a crowd.

''What about Ted?'' Kendra offered. ''Won't he take you?''

''Oh, Ted.'' Patty sank down onto Kendra's sofa and swung her feet up. ''He's so undependable, who knows? Besides, it wouldn't be the same.'' She propped a cushion behind her head and glanced at Kendra. ''So, how is it going with you?''

Kendra gestured toward the sketches spread out on her drawing board. ''Just great, actually. I haven't been so excited about an idea in a long time, and we're going to have no trouble at all selling it. As a matter of fact...''

''Not work, silly, home. How's your husband?''

Kendra hesitated, then grinned. ''As a matter of fact, that's great, too.'' She swung around on her stool to face Patty and thrust her hands into the pockets of her smock, a habit she had that invariably betrayed her enthusiasm for the subject. ''Coming home every night to a fresh-cooked meal, a spotless house, fresh flowers in every room... Do you know he actually bought new towels? The big, fluffy kind with satin borders. And sheets, with crocheted lace. I didn't even have to ask him, he just did. And he had deadbolts installed on all my doors—just dropped the keys by the office one afternoon; I didn't even have to see him.

And Maurice—he's a new cat. I guess it has something to do with having someone around the house all day. And the yard looks great. He turns on the sprinklers every day—I didn't even know I *had* sprinklers. Do you know what it's like?" She paused, searching for a metaphor. "It's like that fairy tale—*Beauty and the Beast*?—where she goes into the castle and all her needs are provided for, clothes, food, fine crystal, golden goblets, everything she wants before she even wants it, and she never even sees the beast. That's the best part," Kendra decided with an enthusiastic nod. "I never even see him."

"Sounds like a dream come true," Patty said, her eyes alight with wonder. "I never expected anything like that."

"Me, either. He pays all my bills and goes to the post office and buys the groceries—he even unpacked all those cartons I had stored away in the closets from the move. And it's true what he said—now that I don't have all those stupid details to worry about, I really am doing some of the best work of my life."

Of course, things were not perfectly smooth on the home front, but Kendra had made far too great an investment in her house husband to admit to any problems. It *was* awkward having a man around the house, even if she never saw him, and Kendra found herself spending much more time than she ever had before picking up after herself. She didn't want him to think she was a slob, after all. He had stocked her bar with a fine selection of wines and liquors, but she was afraid to drink any of it lest he measure the contents each morning and decide she was an alcoholic. It had finally occurred to her that he expected her to eat the yogurt for breakfast, so she diligently poured one container down the garbage disposal every morning and had a breakfast of pastries or fast food on the way to the office. All of this, of course, set up a guilt-resentment reaction—who was she trying to impress, anyway? Why didn't she just tell him she hated yogurt? Why was she letting him intimidate her?

On the first morning she left a timid note on the refrigerator: "Michael, please buy cookies."

That night when she came home there was a box of granola bars waiting in plain view on the counter. After a nutritious dinner of broiled sole and steamed vegetables, she left another note: "Please buy Oreo double-fudge cookies and vanilla ice cream."

The next evening there was a note on the refrigerator that read, "Fresh strawberries for dessert."

The next morning she left the following note: "Shopping list: chocolate cookies, vanilla ice cream, hot-fudge sauce, whipped cream, maraschino cherries, Sarah Lee cheesecake, one dozen cupcakes (any flavor), one bag Reese's Pieces, one Boston cream pie."

That night her dinner was a fruit salad.

She bought her own cookies and ate them all in one sitting.

And then there was the matter of the tax forms. Every night he left a note on her desk: "What are you going to do about these?" "Four days until deadline." "Call me at home about this." And last night, in big black underlined letters, "Tomorrow is April 14!"

Every day she reminded herself to call her accountant, and every day she forgot. And it seemed to her the notes were getting a bit testy.

Her thoughts, as always, were reflected on her face, and Patty missed nothing. There was eager curiosity in her eyes as she demanded, "And?"

Kendra drew her attention back to her friend. "And what?"

"And so nothing is that perfect. What gives?"

Kendra shrugged uncomfortably. "Nothing. Everything is fine."

"Come on, I know you better than that." Patty sat up, hot on the scent of a scandal. "What does he do—pad the budget? Drink on the job?"

Kendra frowned. "Of course not."

"Make passes at you? Steal your underwear?"

"Certainly not!"

"Then what?" Patty insisted. "What's wrong?"

Kendra drummed her pencil absently on the drawing board. She would have gladly answered that question if only she had known what the answer was. She had never had it so good. What difference did a box of cookies and a few irritable notes make? None, she decided. None at all.

"You know," she said after a moment. "I think it might be easier if he were a crotchety old man or a teenager with nothing better to do. But there's something about having a man in my own age bracket—healthy, resourceful and fairly intelligent—taking care of my house, cooking my meals, doing my laundry.... It makes me feel, well, weird."

A gleam of an entirely different sort came into Patty's eyes. "Good-looking, huh?"

Kendra was uncomfortable. "Well, I'm not saying he's the twentieth century's answer to Adonis or anything but...yes. He's okay. Better than okay. Maybe even a little sexy."

Patty chortled with laughter. "I love it! Kendra Phillips has got a crush on her maid!"

Kendra scowled. "I do not. Anyway, that has nothing to do with it at all. Stop laughing. Wouldn't *you* feel strange if a more-or-less reasonably attractive member of the opposite sex was living in your house and taking care of your cat and doing all sorts of personal things for you?"

"I would feel—" Patty gave an exaggerated sigh and turned her eyes heavenward "—like a princess."

Kendra's mouth turned down dryly. "Maybe that's the problem. Some of us were meant to be princesses; I think I preferred being a frog."

There was, after all, such a thing as being *too* perfect. And as day after perfect day went by, Kendra couldn't help feeling as though she were waiting for the other shoe to drop.

That very afternoon, her waiting came to an end.

When she arrived home from work there was a blue van parked in her driveway that could only belong to Michael Drake. She was aware of a very definite tingle of excitement mixed in with her curiosity as she got out of the car and went up the walk. Michael opened the door for her as she mounted the steps, and she attributed her irrational nervousness to mere surprise at finding him there.

This was the first time Kendra had seen him in anything other than a business suit and tie. He was wearing a gray sweatshirt, faded jeans, and sneakers with no socks. His sleeves were pushed up over his elbows, revealing strong forearms dusted with hair, and the jeans outlined the muscles of his thighs, which were long and lean. His hair was rumpled, and even his bare ankles seemed sexy to Kendra. His informal dress should have made him seem less formidable, but in fact, his appearance, so casual and at ease in her home, had exactly the opposite effect. And his expression was not very welcoming.

"You're late," he greeted her, and closed the door behind her as she came in.

Kendra was determined to be polite. "This is the time I always get home." She dropped her portfolio on the floor, and Michael immediately picked it up and placed it in the closet. "Why are you still here?"

"I was waiting for you."

Kendra scooped up Maurice and buried her face briefly in his fur to hide her alarm at that statement. "Oh? Why?"

"I wanted to talk to you, and I knew this was the only way I'd be able to do it."

She glanced at him, trying to disguise her anxiety. What could he possibly want to talk to her about? Surely he wasn't going to quit. But from the look on his face, whatever he had on his mind could not be very pleasant.

Maurice began to squirm, and she had to let him go. She felt naked without the cat as a buffer, but she faced Michael with every appearance of nonchalance. "What do you want to talk about?"

"This." He pulled out a stack of papers and snapped them with the back of his hand, his expression grim. Vaguely Kendra recognized her tax forms. "You've ignored every inquiry I've made, and the deadline is now less than thirty-six hours away. Furthermore, your accountant called today—"

"Oh, good," Kendra said, relieved that it was nothing more serious. "Did you ask her to file for an extension?"

"I most certainly did not. I made an appointment for ten o'clock in the morning."

"You shouldn't have done that! I want an extension. I always file for an extension!"

"Not this year you don't," he replied flatly. "There's no excuse for any of my clients to file late. April 15 comes just about this time every year, and you've had plenty of notice. You're going to get your records together and have this return in on time if it takes the rest of the night to do it."

Kendra eye's narrowed with the effort to control her temper. "I *always* file late," she told him. "The local auditor and I are on a first-name basis because I always file late. If I were to file on time it would throw the whole system out of whack, and I, for one, do not care to be responsible for the downfall of the U.S. government. Furthermore," she finished triumphantly, "I don't have time to keep that appointment tomorrow, so you can just call my accountant and cancel it."

"You don't have to keep the appointment," he responded coolly. "I will."

"You're not allowed to do that!"

"I certainly am. All you have to do is give me the information and sign the tax forms. I'll take care of everything else."

Kendra's frustration level rose with every word he spoke. Maurice strolled over to Michael and began to rub against his ankles, and Kendra glared at the cat. *Traitor,* she thought.

She turned her scowl back to Michael. "If you think for one minute that I'm going to spend my evening looking all over this house for bank statements and receipts and little slips of paper—"

"That is exactly what you're going to do." His tone was curt, and Kendra's outrage was only compounded by the spark that kindled in his eyes. "I can't do everything, you know, and I don't think it's too much to ask for a little cooperation from you."

"Cooperation!" she snapped back. "I could use some of that myself!"

His eyes narrowed, though he kept his voice deceptively mild. "In what way?"

"Cookies!" she retorted, completely abandoning the effort to be reasonable for the long-awaited relief of giving vent to the frustrations that had been building over the past week. She placed her hands on her hips and met him glare-for-glare, her eyes blazing. "Every day I leave you a shopping list, and every day you ignore it! I thought grocery shopping was one of your jobs."

"My job is to see that you have what you need," he retorted, "and your diet is perfectly well balanced and nutritionally sound as far as it's in my ability to control."

"Oh, yes, right," she replied sarcastically. "Like a refrigerator full of yogurt! Did it ever occur to you to *ask* whether or not I like yogurt? I hate yogurt!"

"So you get your revenge by ignoring *my* notes about your tax returns," he retorted. "Perfect logic!"

"I told you about the tax returns! I don't want to talk about tax returns. That's not the point at all! The point is *you* work for *me*, remember? You're supposed to do what I tell you to!"

"No," he replied shortly, and there was no mistaking the blaze of anger in his eyes. "I am supposed to do what's best for you. If you want someone to blindly follow your orders, get a robot—or a dog."

"I might be better off, at that!"

He took a step toward her, and she bravely held her ground. "Do you know what your trouble is?" he challenged. "You're threatened by my masculinity."

For a moment Kendra was too flabbergasted to speak. "I'm *what*?"

"I've seen this kind of behavior before," he assured her. "It's typical of overachieving insecure women like yourself. You can't accept that fact that a man can do a better job domestically than you can, so you go out of your way to sabotage me."

"I don't have to sabotage you! You're doing a fine job of that by yourself."

"You're being unreasonable."

"And you're being impossible. You're supposed to be making my life easier, but so far all I've gotten out of this deal is headaches."

"You're bringing it on yourself." He waved the tax forms angrily before her face. "If you'd taken care of this when you were supposed to, you wouldn't be facing a deadline now."

She dismissed the forms with an angry gesture. "When I come home from a hard day at the office the last thing in the world I want to hear about is tax forms, and if you *have* to bring me your problems couldn't it at least wait until after I've had a drink? And another thing—" she took a breath, glaring at him. "—I *hate* coming home to a fight!"

For a moment they stood there, toe-to-toe, eyes locked and fists clenched, the immovable object and the irresistible force. His eyes were churning and hers were snapping, her hands were planted on her hips and his jaw was thrust forward belligerently. And then, almost at the same moment, they became aware of the humor of their position—the typical couple locked in mortal combat over domestic trivia. His lips began to twitch with mirth, and Kendra tightened her own against a smile. He looked sexy when he was angry, she decided.

After a moment she said, "Are we having our first fight?"

Humor won out, tugging one corner of his mouth downward with a dry smile. "Afraid so. Shall we start over?"

She relaxed her posture, giving way to the amusement that bubbled through. "Hi, honey, I'm home."

He grinned and flung an arm lightly around her shoulders, walking with her toward the living room. "Hard day at the office, dear?"

"Oh, the usual. How about you? What did you do all day?"

"Cooking, cleaning, shopping . . . the usual."

Kendra chuckled. "We're a pretty boring couple. What do married people find to talk about?"

He glanced down at her meaningfully. "Tax forms."

She groaned.

"I'll tell you what," he offered quickly, before she could say anything. "How about a compromise? I'll make a chocolate mousse for dinner, and you start looking for last year's tax records."

She did not have the faintest idea where to begin to look, but for the promise of chocolate mousse and no more arguing, it was worth a try. "Maybe in my desk?" she suggested.

He shook his head, starting toward the kitchen. "I've looked there."

"What about those cartons in the upstairs closet?"

"I've already unpacked them. Nothing there."

"Maybe..." she began, but he was in the kitchen, and the problem was hers.

Michael was no more surprised than Kendra when she found the records twenty minutes later—in a shoebox in the utility shed, wedged between a broken Exercycle and a box of empty baby food jars that she sometimes used for mixing paint. She deposited the shoebox triumphantly on the desk and, as an added courtesy, signed the tax forms he had left there.

She dusted off her hands and grimaced at the state of her clothes, which were grubby from crawling around in the shed. "I'm going to take a shower," she called to Michael.

"Dinner's in half an hour," he returned.

Kendra grinned as she called back, "That's the way you're supposed to greet me after a hard day at the office."

She heard him chuckling, and she felt absurdly happy as she started up the stairs.

Five

It occurred to Kendra that for the first time in quite a while she would be having dinner alone with a man. She had had her share of dates and the requisite number of dinners with clients and associates at which nothing was discussed but business and after which one of them would pick up the check and deduct it as a business expense. But this was different. She felt excited and anticipatory about spending an evening alone with Michael in a way she couldn't explain, nor did she try.

She showered quickly, wrapped herself in one of the fluffy new towels that Michael had bought, then stood for a long time in front of her closet, trying to decide what to wear. She pulled out a slinky little skirt and midriff top that she had never had the courage to wear before and thought it might be just the thing to disabuse Michael of any notions he might have that she was fat. Then she held the outfit up before the mirror, remembered why she had never worn it and decided not to push her luck.

She hesitated over an attractive peach-flowered print with handkerchief sleeves and a long swinging skirt; it flattered her figure and was very stylish, but she thought it might be a bit too elegant for the occasion. She never felt comfortable in jeans, and her breasts were too small to look good in a T-shirt. Then she was irritated with herself for worrying about what her breasts would look like to Michael Drake and determinedly put the entire matter into perspective. This wasn't a date, after all.

She finally chose a colorful cotton mumu with a scooped neck and petal sleeves. The cut was just full enough to soften her figure without disguising it, and the bold colors looked good on her. She finger-brushed her damp hair into gentle curls and applied a light tracing of lipstick, but her naturally dramatic dark eyes needed no enhancement. In honor of the occasion, she even wore shoes.

Michael was turning from the stove when she came into the kitchen, and the quick appreciative light that sprang into his eyes made her instantly glad she had spent time on her appearance. But in another moment sharp hunger pangs pushed aside other concerns, and she exclaimed, "It smells wonderful! What are we having?"

"Beef stroganoff." He centered a plate of steaming noodles and beef on the place mat and invited, "Sit down. I'll pour the wine."

She noticed then that the table was set for only one. "You're not eating?"

"No, I'm going to start sorting through those records and try to get it finished tonight. I'll eat when I get home."

"You haven't seen that box yet. You'd better eat now."

He set a glass of rich burgundy on the table. "I'll hold out."

This was not working out at all the way she had expected, and Kendra was irrationally disappointed. She pointed out, without taking her seat, "It's rude to make me eat alone."

He hesitated, and then explained, "I told you before, I don't socialize with clients."

"Oh, for heaven's sake," she responded impatiently. "I'm not asking you for a date. It's just dinner." And a taunting little voice in the back of her mind echoed, *Just dinner? Then why did you spend twenty minutes trying to decide what to wear and put on lipstick and shoes?* She ignored the voice.

Michael thought for a moment then decided, "All right. I suppose we could use the time to discuss business."

Kendra rolled her eyes but wisely kept silent.

While he was busy at the stove Kendra found a box of matches and, on a mischievous whim, lit the candles and dimmed the kitchen light. Michael lifted an eyebrow as he brought his own plate to the table. "Well, well. You're full of surprises, aren't you?"

"So we don't have to look at the mess in the kitchen," she explained, perfectly reasonably, and took her seat.

His lips quirked with an expression she could not read as he murmured, "Of course."

"You really should get some dining-room furniture," he added as he sat down. "Then you'd never have to eat in the kitchen."

"Or patio furniture," she agreed amicably. "This would be a perfect night to dine outside."

"I could take care of that for you."

"Would you?" She picked up on that enthusiastically. "That would be wonderful."

"Tomorrow, if you like," he offered. "All you have to do is pick it out."

She was deflated. "Why can't you do it?"

"You're the decorator, not me," he explained patiently. "You have to tell me what you want. After all, it is your home, and you have to take some responsibility for it."

She opened her napkin in her lap with a disgruntled expression. "I don't see what the big deal is. All you have to do is walk into the store, point to a display and have it delivered."

"Exactly," he responded mildly.

Kendra tasted her wine, holding his gaze. "Pink-and-purple stripes," she told him. "I want pink-and-purple striped patio furniture."

For a moment he made no response. Then he tilted his head slightly in a gesture of concession and picked up his fork.

Kendra turned her attention to her meal. "This is good," she told him. Then, feeling she owed him some sort of apology for her harsh words earlier, she added, "Everything you make is good. How did you learn to cook like this?"

"Necessity," he answered. "I like to eat."

She shrugged. "So do I, but that never inspired me to learn how to cook."

"So I noticed," he murmured dryly.

"There's just one problem," she couldn't help pointing out. "You forgot the bread. And butter."

"I didn't forget. The noodles fulfill your bread requirement, and no one needs extra fat in the diet."

Kendra should have known better than to bring up any subject that could lead to the word "diet," but she was too far into the conversation to retreat now. The best thing to do was to face it head on and dispense with the matter once and for all.

She put down her fork, touched her napkin to her lips and commanded calmly, "Michael, look at me."

He did.

"Do you think I'm fat?"

His surprise seemed genuine. "Why, no. You have a terrific figure." She liked the way his gaze skated downward as he added with a touch of amusement, "What I can see of it."

Her pleasure with the compliment—and with the look in his eyes—almost overrode her determination to make her point. Almost, but not quite. "Then why," she demanded plainly, "do you keep me on these starvation portions?"

"It has nothing to do with calories," he explained patiently. "It has to do with nutrition. As long as your health is my responsibility—"

"I know, I know." She flung up a hand in exasperation. "Yogurt, fresh fruit—gerbil food! But I can't live on that. It so happens that sometimes the only thing I get for breakfast is coffee..." A slight exaggeration there, but she didn't care. "And I never eat lunch—"

"Why not?" he interrupted, concerned.

"Because I just don't, that's all."

"You could come home for lunch."

"I don't want to come home for lunch," she replied impatiently. His utterly humorless, stubbornly involved approach to the subject was beginning to get on her nerves. All she had wanted was to make a simple request. "It's too much trouble, it interrupts my train of thought and I don't have time. Anyway—"

"You really should eat lunch," he advised soberly. "Skipping meals is a very bad health practice."

"*Anyway,*" she overrode him firmly, "That's not the point. All I'm trying to say is that I need real food. Fat, sugar, cholesterol, *calories*, for goodness sake! Is that too much to ask?"

He looked at her gravely. "If you get started on a regimen like that, you'll regret it five years down the road. Women's bodies metabolize differently, you know, and as you approach thirty—"

"I am not thirty!" she exclaimed, at the end of her patience. "And what do you know about women's bodies, anyway?"

He almost managed to hide the roguish sparkle in his eyes. "Oh, enough to get by," he admitted modestly.

She looked at him narrowly as slow suspicion solidified into certainty, and outrage took its place. "You're making fun of me!" she accused. "You've done that before! One minute you're acting like the most arrogant, boorish, conceited ass that ever walked the earth and the next you're laughing at me, and I never can tell which is which. And I'll tell you something else—I don't like it one bit!"

She sat there, glaring at him, while he lifted his glass to cover his laughter. "I'm sorry," he admitted, his eyes dancing. "But it's hard to resist sometimes. You're just too easy to tease."

She liked the laughter in his eyes and the line that appeared along his cheek when he was trying not to grin, and those two factors went a long way toward soothing her injured dignity. Watching him, sitting across from her so relaxed and undeniably masculine, caused a thrill to start in her stomach that was totally inappropriate for the moment.

She demanded, somewhat grudgingly, "Are you always teasing when you act like a jerk?"

He thought about that. "No," he decided. "I wasn't teasing when I met you at the door this evening."

"A moment that will live in infamy," she muttered, and had the pleasure of hearing him chuckle.

She picked up her fork again and declared, "I know why you took this job. To torture me, right? Your own life was dull and unfulfilling so you thought you'd spice it up by seeing how miserable you could make mine, right?"

"Nope." He was watching her with an easy pleasure that made her skin tingle. "That's not it."

"Then it was a practical joke that Patty came up with and talked you into."

He shook his head. "Wrong again."

"Then why?" She looked at him, genuinely curious now. "You could have sent any one of your employees here, you didn't have to do it yourself. You didn't even have to take the job at all. So why did you?"

A speculative light came into his eyes as his gaze went over her, and she felt her body respond instinctively—and probably irrationally—to his look. There was a catch in her throat, a warmth to her skin and a tightening in her abdomen that felt absurdly like anticipation. Then he murmured, "I don't think I'm going to tell you that . . . yet."

And that, of course, was the one thing he could have said that was guaranteed to sharpen Kendra's curiosity. That and the secretively exciting way he looked at her. She put down her fork deliberately and announced, "No, you don't. I'm not eating another bite until you tell me why you took this job."

The amusement was back in his eyes, the moment was gone. He tilted his glass to her in a small salute. "Because you're so much fun to tease," he answered.

Kendra felt the glow of his humor spread over her, and she could no longer prevent the quirky grin of pleasure that broke across her lips. She thought, *I like you, Michael Drake. You make me crazy, you infuriate me, you've turned my life upside-down . . . but I could definitely get used to having you around.*

Michael cleared the table as she finished her wine, and Kendra sat there, taking pleasure in simply watching him move. After a moment she inquired, "Where do you live?"

"In Pleasant Hills. About five miles from here."

"In an apartment or a house?"

A corner of his lips tightened dryly as he took her meaning. "An apartment," he admitted.

She nodded with the superior air of a prosecuting attorney. "And I'll bet *you* don't eat yogurt for breakfast."

"No," he conceded, "but I do work out and play racquetball and swim five miles a day."

"There's nothing more boring than fitness freaks."

He closed the refrigerator door and leaned against it, his hands open in a gesture of conciliation. "All right," he grinned, "Point taken. What do you like for breakfast?"

"Egg McMuffins," she responded immediately.

His humor faded. "Try again."

"Fruit Loops."

He gave a barely perceptible wince. "Maybe we can work something out."

She liked talking to him, watching his expression change, engaging him in playful banter and hearing the sound of his voice. She couldn't recall ever knowing anyone who gave her such pleasure in simple conversation before, and she wanted to pursue it. "What do you really do all day?" she inquired curiously. "Do you spend all your time here, at my house?"

He began to load the dishwasher. "Of course not. There's barely enough to keep me busy here for a couple of hours."

"Then what?"

"I do have an office to run," he reminded her.

"And working out to do and racquetball to play and miles to swim," she finished. "Do you have a girl-friend?"

"You ask too many questions."

"How else am I supposed to get to know you?"

"You're not supposed to know me," he informed her, taking her plate to the sink. "I'm supposed to be a shadowy figure in the back of your life, like the postman or the meter reader. Somebody you don't even think about until something goes wrong."

"Aha," she murmured. "So it's part of your job to be mysterious, too."

"Not mysterious." He rinsed her plate and placed it in the dishwasher. "Just practical. It doesn't pay to get too close to the clients."

She tilted her head speculatively. "Company policy, or personal?"

He turned, regarding her for a moment with an expression that almost could have held a gentle warning. "Maybe both."

"I see." She nodded sagely. "You're afraid your clients will fall in love with you."

He grinned unexpectedly and came over to her, bending close as he removed her empty wineglass from her fingers. "How could they resist?"

Kendra tilted her head toward his, and though her tone was as playful as his, her pulse speeded with his nearness. "Maybe easier than you think, Mr. Wonderful."

He laughed and straightened up. "You're very good at this."

"At what?"

"Flirting." He flashed a glance at her as he bent to place her glass in the dishwasher. "But don't waste your talent on me, okay? I already think you're adorable."

Her heart skipped, and something inside her soared absurdly. *Adorable.* He thought she was adorable. She wanted to pursue that—how badly she wanted to pursue that!—but all she could think of to say was, "Don't I get any more wine?"

He closed and locked the dishwasher. "Not tonight. We have business to discuss."

She groaned and pushed herself out of her chair. "I should have known." She squared her shoulders and faced him. "All right. Let's get it over with."

He turned, drying his hands on a dishtowel. "Quite simply," he informed her, "I can't do my job unless I start getting some more input from you."

Her expression reflected her dismay. "Don't start that again."

"Look at this place," he insisted, waving his hand. "When you start entertaining, your collection of jelly glasses and chipped stoneware isn't going to go very far. Don't you think it's about time you invested in some crystal and china? And I thought we agreed you were going to redecorate. Your television and stereo are on their last legs, and you should really start all over with a built-in entertainment system—not to mention that great library and solarium that are just going to waste. How long are you going to live in this house without window coverings? That's a security risk, if nothing else. And speaking of security, you know you need to have an alarm system installed. I could go on. The bottom line is that until you give me a house to manage, Kendra, you're just wasting my time and your money. We need to get moving on this thing."

She shifted her weight uncomfortably. "I'll get around to it."

"When?" he insisted. "Why are you procrastinating?"

She sighed, casting her eyes around the room briefly as though in search of an answer. "Oh...I don't know. Crystal, china, drapery patterns— It all seems so permanent. Like something my mother would do."

His smile held an unexpected touch of compassion. "Time to grow up, huh?"

She shrugged. "I guess."

"We all face it sometime."

"Then why do you still live in an apartment?" she challenged. And then she sighed. "All right. Buy crystal and china. And flatware, too, while you're at it."

His expression was patient. "Pick out a pattern."

She groaned again. "This *is* worse than getting married."

He grinned. "Depends on your point of view."

She threw up her hands helplessly. "All right. I'll pick out a pattern."

"That's a beginning," he responded cheerfully. "Go ahead and get started. I'll bring coffee and dessert into the living room."

It took Kendra precisely five minutes to locate her pattern books and randomly check off selections. If she had been so cavalier about decorating her client's homes, she would not have lasted five minutes in the business, and the expression on Michael's face when she defiantly showed him her choices suggested that he knew it. But wisely, the only comment he made was, "There. That wasn't so painful, was it?"

She had to admit it was not.

Michael did not share the chocolate mousse with her but took his coffee to her desk and immediately went to work on the shoebox. Watching him made Kendra so nervous that she could barely enjoy the rich confection. The evening had gone so smoothly that she dreaded testing his patience with her system of record keeping, and after a moment she offered hesitantly, "I'm not sure I like the idea of your going through all my personal papers like that. Maybe I should do it myself."

He cast her a dry look over his shoulder. "Kendra Phillips," he said, "I've washed your underwear; I

don't think you have any reason to be shy about what
I might find in this box."

Nonetheless she barely restrained herself long
enough to finish the mousse. Then she took her coffee cup and hovered over his shoulder, wincing every
time he uncovered some meaningless scrap of paper,
snatching personal letters from his hand, offering
helpful—or more often, hindering—advice on where
this might be found or the other might be hidden until finally he looked up at her in exasperation and
suggested, "Don't you have something to do?"

Chagrined and more or less defeated, Kendra went
in search of something to do.

She flipped through magazines, she turned the television on and then off again, she picked up a book.
But repeatedly her attention kept straying to Michael—the way the fabric of his pants stretched taut
across his thighs, the way his hair swept the back of his
neck; the way his dark brows knotted in concentra-
tion and then cleared in comprehension or the way the
lamplight shadowed his strong forearm as he moved
pen across paper. He had large hands, she observed,
strong and competent and outdoor bronze. She wondered if his hands would be soft to the touch or
roughened from the work he did. She had never
known a man with workman's hands.

He thought she was adorable. What did that mean?
Why did her stomach tighten with a silly pleasure
whenever she remembered it?

Trouble, she told herself firmly. *That's what it
means. More trouble than you want to handle if you
don't stop fantasizing and remember who he is and
what he's doing here and that that's where it begins
and ends.*

And on that stern note she got her portfolio from
the closet, cleared off the coffee table and spread out
her work. After a few false starts—once to remove
Maurice from the center of her sketches and once or
twice to glance at Michael—she settled down on the
floor, took up her drawing pens and in no time at all
was immersed in what she loved best.

The hours that passed were comfortable in a way
Kendra had never known an evening at home to be.
Only once did Michael pause to mutter, mostly to
himself, "If you ran your business like you run your
personal finances, you'd be bankrupt inside a year."
And Kendra only smiled. There was something pleasantly soothing about having him there, sitting at her
desk and putting her life in order while she indulged
herself in the pleasures of her own work. It felt right
and natural. It was good not to be alone.

The project Kendra was working on was nick-
named "The-Sun-Never-Sets-on-the-British-Empire
House." It had begun as a whim, but the more she
worked on it the more excited she became about it.
Most of Dream Houses's concepts were traditional or
ultramodern in design, with an occasional foray into
the bizarre for a particularly eccentric client; it was a
refreshing change to work on something rooted in
history and authenticity. The basic scheme was Victorian, but each room reflected a different aspect of
that age and a slightly different tone: the formal elegance of the foyer with its ponderous grandfather
clock flowed into a great room designed to suggest a
Victorian parlor with heavy scrolled furniture, bro-
cade chairs and many scarved tables cluttered with
knickknacks. Without realizing it, she incorporated
Michael's suggestion of a built-in entertainment sys-

tem hidden in a reproduction armoir, for one of the trademarks of Dream Houses was that they should be functional as well as attractive.

Contrasting with the busy, overdone parlor was the sun room, representing an English garden with its myriad plants and white wicker furniture cushioned with chintz and light flowery prints; the library, which was modeled after a gentleman's club, in deep wine and leather; the sleek Oriental lines of the formal dining room; the earthy tones of an Irish farmland kitchen; the Egyptian motif of the guest bath and the Colonial India theme of the master bedroom, with its lazily rotating ceiling fan and pedestal bed draped in yards of gauzy mosquito netting. Each room was different, yet all were unified by color, theme and the late-nineteenth-century motif.

Kendra worked until her eyes burned and her hand cramped, and just when she decided it was time to stop for the night, another detail would come to mind that she had to get on paper before she went to bed. She could hardly wait to get to the office the next morning, to pull out the reference books and pattern samples that would give her ideas form and substance. She would have to go to the library, too, and delve into some history sources....

She didn't even hear Michael the first time he spoke to her. "Kendra?"

She glanced up and was surprised to find him standing over her.

"I said I'm finished," he repeated. "Don't touch anything. I'll be back in the morning to take it all to your accountant."

"Oh. Thanks." She turned back to her sketches. "Good night."

He hesitated. "It's after midnight. Aren't you tired?"

That got her attention. She never stayed up past ten-thirty if she could help it. "Goodness, is it?" She peered at her watch and discovered that it was, indeed, twenty after twelve. "I must've gotten carried away."

She stretched and then grimaced at the sudden cramp in her shoulder. "Ouch!" She tried to rub away the aching spot with her fingers, but couldn't quite reach it.

"It's no wonder." Michael's tone was reproving as he brushed her hand away and took her shoulders in a firm, massaging grip. "Sitting on the floor like that, working in that awkward position for hours. Here, lean your head forward. Relax. Why don't you set up a drawing board in here?"

"Too much trouble. Besides, there's not enough light." His fingers worked her shoulders with strong probing movements; a good touch, firm and confident. She let her head drop forward, stretching the muscles of her neck.

"There's enough light in the solarium," he pointed out. He sat on the couch behind her, applying more pressure to the deep knots of her muscles, and she moaned involuntarily. "Does that hurt?"

"Yes. No. Ouch—yes!"

"Relax. You're fighting me."

His fingertips moved, with a lighter touch now, to the ridges of her cervical spine, his thumbs pressing and releasing in rhythmical movements on either side of the cord of her neck. She tried to relax, but it was hard to do with the sudden awareness of him that was creeping over her. His fingertips were calloused, and his touch was warm and purposeful and energizing. His knees were on either side of her, brushing her rib cage as he sat above her on the low couch, and she felt surrounded by him, swaying with the movements of his hands.

She managed, after a moment, "I should be doing this for you. You've been working as long as I have."

"Ah, but I'm tougher."

"Besides—" she drew in a soft, appreciative breath as his hands moved back to her shoulders, heating the skin through the material of her dress and then soothing it with long, penetrating strokes "—it's your job."

She sensed, rather than saw, the smug smile in his voice. "No. This is a bonus."

How good it was to be touched by a man. She had almost forgotten the sensation of strength and gentleness in a man's hands, the slow coursing of warmth that seeped through skin and muscles and fibers. She could hear his soft breathing and her own. There was a tightening in her stomach when his fingertips touched her bare skin, moving gently now, gathering and releasing, then in slow circular, hypnotic strokes that were as sensual as a caress. Her muscles responded to his touch with a will of their own; relaxing and becoming pliant, almost liquid. Her senses were sated with him, replete and glistening with contentment. It was good. So good.

His hands moved down, palms flat, along her back to the indentation of her waist and slowly upwards again. She felt the change come over him as it did her; a deepening awareness, a slow questing intensity. When his hands reached her shoulders a slight pressure drew her backward, closer to him, so that her shoulders were almost resting against his thighs. She could feel his heat, and her breath was suspended. Every nerve was alive with anticipation. His fingers caressed the back of her neck, brushing against the curve of her ear. Her pulses leapt. She knew if she turned her face his would be bent toward her and there would be something in his eyes that had not been there before...the same thing she was feeling now. Her skin prickled and her throat tightened as he trailed a featherlight touch along her collarbone.

And then, almost as though it had never been, the moment was gone. He rested his hands lightly on her shoulders again, and his voice sounded only lightly husky, but unmistakably casual, as he inquired, "What are you working on?"

Kendra released her breath. She tried to match her tone to his as she reached forward to lift a sketch. "A new project. The motif is Victorian—kind of *The Night Before Christmas* meets *Out of Africa*. I'm really excited about it."

He leaned forward to pick up the sketch, and his chest brushed against her shoulders as he did so. She no longer felt comforted by his presence, but trapped, overwhelmed by awareness. She moved away as unobtrusively as possible, beginning to gather up her pens. Her face was hot.

"There's still some coffee left," she offered. "Do you want some?"

"No, thanks." He picked up another sketch, and another, studying them intently. "Do you shop for all the furnishings yourself?"

"Not anymore; we have a shopping service. I used to, though. It was like a treasure hunt. Sometimes if I couldn't find a particular piece, I'd have it custom built, and once or twice I even ended up putting something together myself." Her eyes softened with pleasant reminiscence. "I wish I still had time to do it myself, though. Especially with a house like this; it would really be fun."

A slow secret smile began to play on his lips as he went through the sketches one by one, and then he glanced at her. "You know what you've done, don't you?"

Kendra looked blank.

"This—" he thumped the pile of sketches with his forefinger "—is your house." When she was still uncomprehending, he spread them out for her. "Look. The foyer with the mullioned windows and the grandfather clock. The great room. The solarium you call a sun room. Even the kitchen." Then he looked up at her, grinning. "Your conscious mind may have been fighting getting this place together, but your subconscious has gone ahead and done it for you."

Kendra sat beside him on the sofa and took up the sketches. Puzzlement changed to cautious wonder as she went through them again. "Why," she admitted at last, "I suppose it could be...."

He laughed. "Of course, it is. This is *your* house, Kendra Phillips. And now that we have something to work with, we'll have it looking like one in no time."

She shook her head a little, for some reason she couldn't fully explain, still reluctant. "Seems a shame to waste such a great idea."

His eyes held a curious, slightly probing expression that was perhaps a bit too perceptive. "Don't you think you deserve it?"

Kendra returned her eyes to the sketches, purely to avoid his gaze. "I guess. I mean, sure. I would love living in a house like this," she admitted, almost catching his enthusiasm. "I suppose it is sort of an conglomeration of everything I've ever wanted to have, but..." And then she sighed, putting the sketches aside. "You have no idea how long it would take and how much trouble it would be, looking up pattern numbers, ordering furnishings, picking out fabric, hours on the phone talking to wholesalers and custom retailers...." She repressed a shudder. "It's just not worth it if there's no profit involved."

He was thoughtful. "And what would the procedure be if you were designing this house to sell?"

"Well...I'd take the sketches to one of my assistants and have her draw up a list, which I'd approve, then we'd turn it over to the shopping service, and I'd approve all their purchases, then someone else would deal with the painters and the wallpaper hangers and the carpenters, and I'd approve all of that. But I can't use company employees like that. It's too expensive, and Patty would kill me."

He nodded. "Especially when you're paying me to do exactly the same thing. So I'll deal with your assistant and the wholesalers and the carpenters and painters and everyone else in between. You won't have to be involved at all, at least not in the first stages."

"Well..." Kendra felt as though she were being backed into a corner.

"I'll bet you could have draperies by the first of next week," he suggested.

Temptation again. Did he have any idea how hard he was to resist? "I suppose," she agreed at last, reluctantly, "we could at least use these sketches as a starting point and move very slowly."

His eyes crinkled with a smile as he dropped his arm around her shoulders and squeezed briefly. "Good girl. You're going to come through this just fine, I promise you."

Her lips tightened into a grudging smile, and she glanced up at him. His arm around her shoulders was warm and easy, his eyes traced with indulgent mirth. His face was close, his eyes the color of a deep-water lake. Something happened to her breathing as she looked at him, and to his. The moment was very still.

Then the embrace of his arm relaxed into a brief impersonal pat on the shoulder, and he stood. "I'd say we accomplished a lot tonight, wouldn't you?" he said lightly, starting for the door.

"Yes." Her voice sounded a little dazed, and she cleared her throat. She gestured to the desk, forcing the same negligence into her tone she had heard in his. "Taxes, home furnishings . . . you're going to turn me into a regular person despite myself."

Once again his smile softened and seemed to linger, as he looked at her. "I wouldn't want to do that," he answered. "I like you just the way you are."

And then, before she had a chance to react, he turned toward the door and added casually, "Good night, then, and be sure to lock up behind me."

Six

The next week was a series of ups and downs. On the up side, Michael replaced the yogurt in her refrigerator with blueberry muffins, and her mornings got off to a much sunnier start. He also left a container of what appeared to be trail mix with the note, "This is not gerbil food. Take it to work with you; it's better than no lunch at all." That made her smile, and she complied. To her surprise, it was actually good, and that night she left him a note: "Michael—I like the gerbil food. Please make some more."

He obviously wasn't going to give in on the cookies, but three nights out of five she discovered something sweet to top off the evening meal, and she felt she was making progress.

She came home one evening and found her patio had been furnished with an umbrella table, chaises and chairs upholstered in pale-pink-and-lavender stripes.

PLAY
SILHOUETTE'S

LUCKY HEARTS
GAME

AND YOU COULD GET

- ★ FREE BOOKS
- ★ A FREE CLOCK/CALENDAR
- ★ A FREE SURPRISE GIFT
- ★ AND MUCH MORE

**TURN THE PAGE AND
DEAL YOURSELF IN** →

PLAY "LUCKY HEARTS" AND YOU COULD GET...

★ Exciting Silhouette Desire® novels—FREE
★ A Lucite Clock/Calendar—FREE
★ A surprise mystery gift that will delight you—FREE

THEN CONTINUE YOUR LUCKY STREAK WITH A SWEETHEART OF A DEAL

When you return the postcard on the opposite page, we'll send you the books and gifts you qualify for, absolutely free! Then, you'll get 6 new Silhouette Desire® novels every month, delivered right to your door months before they're available in stores. If you decide to keep them, you'll pay only $2.24* per month, a savings of 26 cents off the cover price, and there is <u>no</u> charge for postage and handling! You can cancel at any time by marking "cancel" on your statement or returning a shipment to us at our cost.

★ Free Newsletter!
You'll get a free newsletter—an insider's look at our most popular authors and their upcoming novels.

★ Special Extras—Free!
When you subscribe to Silhouette Books, you'll also get additional free gifts from time to time as a token of our appreciation for being a home subscriber.

*Terms and prices subject to change.

FREE LUCITE CLOCK/CALENDAR

You'll love this Lucite clock/calendar—it is a handsome addition to any decor! The changeable month-at-a-glance calendar pops out and can be replaced with your favorite photograph. And it could be YOURS FREE when you play "LUCKY HEARTS!"

DETACH AND MAIL CARD TODAY

SILHOUETTE'S

With a coin — scratch off the silver card and check below to see how many gifts you get.

YES! I have scratched off the silver card. Please send me all the books and gifts for which I qualify. I understand that I am under no obligation to purchase any books, as explained on the opposite page. If I'm not fully satisfied I can cancel at any time but if I choose to continue in the Reader Service, I'll pay the low members-only price each month.

225 CIS JAYU

NAME		
ADDRESS		APT.
CITY	STATE	ZIP

Twenty-one gets you 4 free books, a free clock/ calendar and mystery gift

Twenty gets you 4 free books and a free clock/calendar

Nineteen gets you 4 free books

Eighteen gets you 2 free books

Terms and prices subject to change. All orders subject to approval. Offer limited to one per household and not valid to current Silhouette Desire subscribers.

PRINTED IN U.S.A.

SILHOUETTE "NO RISK" GUARANTEE

★ You're not required to buy a single book—ever!
★ As a subscriber, you must be completely satisfied or you may cancel at any time by marking "cancel" on your statement or returning a shipment of books to us at our cost.
★ The free books and gifts you receive from this LUCKY HEARTS offer remain yours to keep—in any case.

If offer card is missing, write to:
Silhouette Books, 901 Fuhrmann Blvd., P.O. Box 1867, Buffalo, NY 14269-1867

DETACH AND MAIL CARD TODAY

BUSINESS REPLY CARD

First Class   Permit No. 717   Buffalo, NY

Postage will be paid by addressee

Silhouette Reader Service
901 Fuhrmann Blvd.
P.O. Box 1867
Buffalo, NY 14240-9952

NO POSTAGE
NECESSARY
IF MAILED
IN THE
UNITED STATES

She laughed out loud in delight, and that evening spent a peaceful hour outside, sipping a glass of wine and watching the twilight fall. It would have been nicer if she had had someone to share it with, though.

The living room draperies arrived. At first she loved them. Then she hated them. The color was all wrong, the pattern was too busy, she should have chosen Austrian blinds instead. She was plunged into despair at the enormity of the project she had committed herself to. Within two days, she loved the draperies again, but the dread remained over what lay ahead.

She did not see Michael again. Sometimes she caught herself lingering over coffee in the mornings or coming home early, half hoping he would be there, and she was annoyed with herself when she realized what she was doing. What was the matter with her? Whenever they were together a fight was inevitable. He was taking over enough of her life as it was. The last thing she needed was to complicate the situation by spending time with him in person. Yet the memory of the evening they had spent together was vivid, tantalizing her like a promise that had not been quite fulfilled, and she thought about him more than she should have.

It wasn't, she assured herself, that she was really interested in Michael Drake personally. Kendra had come to the realization long ago that, for herself, at least, men were far more trouble than they were worth. She didn't like the game playing, the power tests, the roller-coaster ups and downs of intimate relationships; her love life was therefore sporadic if not Spartan. And even if she had been in the market for a romance, Michael Drake was far from a likely candidate. No, it wasn't that she was personally interested in him. It was just that . . . he was interesting. And she thought it was somewhat odd that, after having spent an entire evening together—an evening that had been sprinkled with more than one expectant moment—he should now be going out of his way to become the invisible man.

On Saturday she went to work as usual. Michael prepared her weekend meals in advance, and Saturday night was long and boring. On Sunday she let Patty talk her into going to a craft show upstate, and when she returned home late Sunday evening there was a message on her answering machine. Her heart skipped at the first mellifluous sounds of a male voice. "Kendra, it's Michael Drake. Just checking to make sure you're using your leisure time wisely. I hope you're out getting some sun and exercise. Enjoy your day off."

The beep of the machine indicated the end of the message, and Kendra stared at it, frustrated. She wondered what Michael would have had to say to her if she had been home to answer the phone.

She kept expecting him to call her or meet her at home, to consult about the decorating project. But he kept his word and kept her out of it. The new sofa and two new chairs arrived. She did her best to ignore them. Each day she came home and something new had been added; piece by piece the trappings of permanence were creeping into her house, cluttering up her life and tying her down. And with each new rug, each small table, her anxiety quotient rose.

"Well for heaven's sake," Patty told her in exasperation at last, "if you don't like the arrangement, call it off. You're paying the bills, aren't you? You told me yourself you've got three months to fire him without losing a penny."

Kendra was appalled. "I don't want to fire him!"

"Then why are you coming in here every morning telling me your problems? It sounds to me like you have the best of all possible worlds."

"Just like Beauty and the Beast," Kendra responded glumly.

Patty glanced at her askance. "From what I hear, he's not exactly a beast. And you're a wimp."

"Yeah," Kendra responded with a sigh. "I used to think Beauty was a wimp, too, for running away from the castle and all that luxury. Now I'm beginning to know how she felt. Life certainly was a lot simpler before Michael Drake moved in and started making things easier for me."

Patty merely gave her a disparaging look. "You just don't know when you're well off."

And that was the end of Patty's sympathy.

That night as Kendra got into bed, irritably plumping up pillows that smelled clothesline fresh, Maurice jumped up on the bed and began his customary discriminating search for the softest place to settle down for the night. She glared at him. "Why aren't you out prowling about like an ordinary tomcat? Can't you get a date, either?"

Maurice gave her a superior look and curled up on the pillow next to her face, purring loudly. Kendra grimaced and brushed the fur away from her face, then turned off the light with a resigned sigh. "That's the trouble around here," she grumbled. "Everyone's too domesticated."

She was awakened in the middle of the night by a loud boom of thunder. She lay there blinking in alarm, until a flash of lightning and another boom assured her that it was, indeed, only a storm that had awakened her. Rain roared like an ocean outside. She groaned and squinted at the clock. The digital numbers were dark and blank. The power was off.

Thunder rolled again, and she turned over, starting to pull the pillow over her ears. Something cold and wet splashed on her face. She stiffened, fully awake now, and another drop splattered on her hand. She sat bolt upright in bed, indignant and alarmed. "The roof is leaking!"

She flung back the covers and started to get out of bed when another flash of lightning burst across the room and froze her in place. Illuminated by the two-second flare was something small and furry at the foot of her bed, staring at her with beady eyes.

She would have screamed if she'd had the breath. She jerked the covers up to her chin and stared, paralyzed, until the lightning came again, and it was still there: a small brown animal with a long tail and glinting eyes, crouched on the floor not two feet away from her.

"Maurice!" she hissed trying to raise her voice to a squeal. "A mouse!"

The cat yawned and stretched and curled himself into a tighter ball, one forepaw hiding his head.

Kendra fumbled for the switch of the lamp, and nothing happened. Her heart was pounding. She couldn't stay in bed with a mouse crawling about. Hadn't she heard somewhere that mice could leap incredible heights and wiggle through places half their size? She thought of that mouse nibbling at her bedcovers, scrambling up the mattress, skittering across her face, and she shuddered, barely repressing a real scream this time.

She grabbed Maurice and flung back the covers. Then she thought of putting her bare feet on the floor, of stumbling across a tiny furry body, of sharp claws scuttling across her toes, and she quickly jerked the covers back again. Maurice meowed sleepily in annoyance. "Stupid cat," she whispered breathlessly, her eyes frantically, unwillingly searching the room. "If you did your job we wouldn't have this problem. What kind of a cat are you, anyway?"

Another drop of rain splattered on her hair, and she knew she couldn't stay there. At the same moment a lightning flash strobed at the creature on the floor, and with a muffled squeal Kendra leapt out of bed and dashed for the door. She slammed it shut and leaned against it, her chest heaving, a squirming Maurice tucked under one arm. Then she jumped away. A mouse could easily squeeze under the doorframe, and hadn't she heard somewhere that if you see one mouse there are probably a hundred others hiding behind the walls? And here she was standing in her bare feet in the dark with hundreds, perhaps thousands, of mice scurrying about.

Holding Maurice so tightly he yowled in protest, Kendra picked her way through the dark to the guest room across the hall, where she stored her winter clothes. With every nerve in her body screaming, she fumbled through the closet until she found a pair of snow boots and, balancing on one foot at a time, pulled them on. Thus armed, she carried Maurice back out into the hallway and paused to catch her breath. That was not easy to do. Her heart was going like a jackhammer, and every time the thunder crashed, she jumped and had to muffle a squeal.

"All right," she whispered, trying to calm herself with the sound of her own voice. It did no good. Her breath was coming in gasps, and her eyes were darting frantically through the dark. "I can deal with this. Mice. Who do you call about mice?"

The obvious answer occurred to her, and again she spoke out loud, forcing firmness into her tone. "No. I am a grown-up competent woman. I deal with hundreds of thousands of dollars every day. Giants of industry come to me for advice. Politicians and kings rely on my judgment. I can deal with this. It's only a mouse, after all."

But she hated mice. Almost as much as she hated squirrels.

The first order of business, she decided, was to find a flashlight. She couldn't stand here in the dark all night. First she would get some light, then she would decide what to do.

Moving clumsily in the heavy boots, holding on to the rail with her free hand, she carefully felt her way downstairs. Maurice hated being carried downstairs, and he scratched her. Kendra did not let him go. The one thing she didn't need was a mouse massacre at the paws of an angry cat. Not that Maurice seemed interested in massacring anything other than her arm.

She couldn't find a flashlight. She didn't even know if she owned a flashlight. She wondered if her bedroom would be flooded by the rainstorm before morning. Certainly the bedding would be ruined. Mouse or no mouse, she had to move the bed away from the leak. How was she supposed to move that heavy bed by herself? How could she go back into the bedroom knowing that mouse was there, crouching in a corner and waiting to spring on her?

She found a box of matches, lit one of the candles on the kitchen table, and carried it unsteadily into the living room. Every time the thunder sounded, the candlelight wavered so badly in her hand that she was afraid she would drop it. She placed the candle on the coffee table and stood there in its meager pool of light, clutching a very dissatisfied Maurice, trying to decide what to do. "I can handle this," she said through clenched teeth, squeezing her eyes closed as thunder rattled the windowpanes. "I can."

But almost before that roll of thunder passed, another one sounded, accompanied by a crash and a crack that illuminated the entire room with a brilliant blue-white glare. Maurice yowled and leapt from her arms. Kendra moved with the same speed, a cry muffled in her throat as she ran to her desk and snatched up her purse.

She scrambled through the contents of her purse—that was one thing Michael had not been able to organize, to her desperate regret at the moment—until she found what she was looking for: the business card with Michael Drake's home number scrawled on the back. For a moment she clutched it in her hand, determined not to do this thing. She was a grown-up, independent woman. She couldn't go running to Michael every time something went wrong. This was *her* problem, and she could handle it. Besides, it was the middle of the night. She couldn't call him in the middle of the night.

But he had said to use the number in case of emergency. If this wasn't an emergency, she didn't know what was.

"I hate this," she muttered. "I'm not going to do this."

A gust of wind flung rain against the windows with deafening force, and she didn't delay another moment. She dragged the telephone over to the light of the candle and punched out the numbers on the card.

It rang once, then twice. Kendra took slow, deep breaths. She wasn't going to sound like a hysterical woman. She wasn't going to give him the impression she couldn't take care of herself. She wasn't going to talk to him at all. She was going to hang up.

Michael's sleepy voice answered.

She took another deep breath. "Michael? This is Kendra Phillips."

She had a sudden vision of him in bed, naked from the waist up, his hair tousled, his expression blurred with sleep. She wondered if he was alone, and then she was filled with chagrin. What if he wasn't alone?

"Kendra?" His voice sharpened a little. "What time is it? Are you all right?"

She took another breath. All right. Calm. Businesslike. "I'm sorry to call you so late," she said, and that was good. Just the right note of detached nonchalance, perfectly professional. "I'm afraid I don't know what time it is; the power is off here. I just wanted to ask a question."

"A question?" There was a rustling and creaking in the background, as though he were sitting up. She could hear the frown in his voice, confused and partially incredulous. She imagined he did not get too many calls in the middle of the night just to ask him a question.

"Yes." She cleared her throat, feeling utterly foolish now and trying with all her might to keep her jangled nerves from revealing themselves in her voice. "It's nothing, really. It's just that my roof is leaking and soaking my bed and there's a mouse in the bedroom, and I was just wondering—what should I do?"

Oh, how helpless and timid that sounded! She hated herself, but she hated it even more when thunder crashed and static popped in her ear. She held the telephone away from her face, wincing.

"—what about the cat?" Michael was saying.

Her careful control almost snapped. "I don't want my cat eating mice!"

"How bad is the leak?"

Lightning struck again, and she had heard about people being electrocuted over the phone. "Bad!" she shouted, all control gone now.

"I'll be right over."

She knew she should protest; that was not why she had called him, she was certain it wasn't. But he had already hung up, and she was glad.

She found Maurice and paced the floor with the cat in her arms until headlights flashed on her window twenty minutes later. She ran to the door and flung it open, watching urgently as Michael ran through the torrent to her doorstep.

His hair was a shiny helmet plastered to his skull, his face was dripping and his trenchcoat was dark and soaked. He took one look at Kendra, standing in her short nightgown and snow boots, clutching the cat to her chest like a deadly weapon, and he burst out laughing.

Kendra endured the onslaught stoically, squaring her shoulders and standing tall against humiliation, and when his amusement had faded to mere chuckles she said coolly, "I didn't ask you to come over, you know."

He made an effort to sober his expression, though mirth still danced crazily in his eyes. "No, you didn't," he admitted. "May I come in?"

She hesitated, wishing she could slam the door in his face and stalk away, but she was hardly in a position to do that. She stepped away from the door, and he came inside. Still holding on to her dignity with both hands, she informed him, "I just want you to know I am not a hysterical woman. I've been taking care of my own life for a great many years now, and I don't have to run to a man whenever I have a problem. When I lived in my apartment I never had to ask anyone for anything. I'm perfectly capable of taking care of myself."

"Of course, you are," he replied soothingly. She could tell it was still a struggle for him to keep a straight face. He slipped off his raincoat, took a flashlight from his pocket, and flicked it on.

She glared at the perfectly innocent instrument of light as though it were the source of all her problems. "*You* have a flashlight!" she accused. "I'm in the middle of a power failure and all I have is candles!"

"You have two flashlights," he informed her. "One in the left-hand drawer next to the stove, and one in your nightstand."

"Now you tell me!"

He hung his raincoat onto the coat stand and started toward the stairs. "The mouse is in the bedroom?"

Dread went through her, and she held Maurice more tightly. He gave a muffled meow. "Do you want me to come with you?" she volunteered hesitantly.

He gave her a thoughtful look over his shoulder. "I think I can take him on my own," he decided gravely. "But I'll call you if there's any trouble."

Kendra whirled away angrily as he started up the stairs, the sound of his soft chuckles echoing even above the rain.

Maurice escaped her again, and Kendra was left on her own, pacing back and forth in the eerie dance of lightning that flickered through the stained-glass door, casting an occasional anxious glance at the dark well of the stairs, trying not to jump when thunder exploded.

Intermingled with the cacophony of the storm she could hear movement upstairs, the scraping of heavy furniture, the creak of footsteps. Once she even started up the stairs, but changed her mind abruptly. She went into the living room where the candle was and sat down on the new sofa, wrapped her arms around herself and waited anxiously.

It took forever before Michael came down, the beam of the flashlight preceding him in gentle sweeping arcs. "There's not much I can do about the leak until morning," he said. "But I moved your bed and changed the linen. You should be able to sleep there for the rest of the night if the sound of the water dripping in the bucket doesn't bother you. And by the way—" he took something from his pocket and held it in the beam of the flashlight. "Here's your mouse."

Kendra clapped both hands over her mouth too late to stifle a scream. Between his thumb and forefinger Michael held the tail of the small furry creature, swinging it back and forth in the light.

"Kendra..." He came toward her, and she scrambled backward on the sofa, emitting another screech of horror and repulsion through her clenched fingers. He was laughing. "It's a toy!"

He sat down beside her, his eyes dancing, swinging the fake fur mouse before her face. "A cat toy," he explained. "I bought it for Maurice yesterday."

For the space of three, perhaps four heartbeats, she stared at him, her eyes wide with residual horror and disbelief. And then with a muffled roar of rage she lunged at him, slapping the toy out of his hand and striking his arm with her closed fist. "You! You crazy person! You think it's funny! I'll show you what's funny! How dare you! You scared me half to death, waking me up in the middle of the night!" That was more truthfully the other way around, but she was too far gone to care much for details. "How dare you!"

He laughingly fended off her blows, finally dropping the flashlight to the sofa between them as he caught her wrists. "Wait just a minute—hold it! I'm one of the good guys, remember?"

She paused, her chest heaving and her wrists captured firmly in his hands, wanting to jerk away and spit more epithets at him even while the rational side of her warned she had already made enough of a fool of herself for one evening. He was very close; she could see the droplets of water that clung to his neck from his wet hair and the dancing warmth in his eyes. The effortless masculine grip he had on her wrists seemed intimate and playful. Her heart was still pounding from the residue of alarm and the outburst of emotions, and now a new tingling heat came to her face, which was probably nothing more than embarrassment over her display.

She held his amused gaze with her narrowed eyes, and she demanded, "You didn't do it on purpose?"

"On my honor," he assured her.

She tugged at her wrists, and he released them with a slowness that could have been caution or reluctance. "I suppose if it had been a real mouse..." she began grudgingly.

"I would have defended you with my life."

She darted him a suspicious look, which slowly, helplessly softened when she met the contagious laughter in his own. Her lips tightened with a reluctant smile. "I guess you think I'm a nut," she mumbled.

"I think I'll reserve comment on that."

She glanced at him, trying hard to stay angry and losing the battle. "You should get a towel and dry your hair," she advised ungraciously.

"I think I will." He stood, taking the flashlight with him. "And," he added, tracing the beam of light down over her bare legs to her feet. "Now that the crisis is over—don't you think you could take off your combat boots?"

She scowled and waited until he was well out of the room before she pulled off her snow boots and placed them well out of sight behind the couch.

He returned in a few moments with a handful of candles in various holders. He had towel-dried his hair to a semifluffy dampness, and the disheveled look suited him. He was wearing faded jeans and a soft blue T-shirt, untucked, unbelted and sexy. She imagined him scrambling out of bed and pulling on his clothes to rush to her rescue, and everything within her softened toward him.

"Something tells me you won't be going back to bed right away," he said as he set up the candles. "There's no point sitting up in the dark."

"Thanks for coming over," she said, in a much more subdued tone than she had used earlier. "I'm sorry I made you get up in the middle of the night and come out in the rain."

"No problem."

She couldn't get the picture of out her mind of him flinging back the bedclothes and pulling jeans over his naked legs, tugging on boots, jerking a T-shirt over his bare chest.... She swallowed. "I hope you weren't busy."

He cast her an incredulous glance as he struck a match. "At two-thirty in the morning?"

"I mean—" again she swallowed uncomfortably. "—if you were with someone...."

He touched the match to the candle, and the glowing yellow light showed an odd expression on his face as he looked at her. "Would it bother you if I was?"

Would it? The very question made her feel foolish and disoriented, and she stammered, "N-no, of course not—I mean, yes, I—I'd be sorry I disturbed you, of course.... I mean, it's none of my business," she finished firmly. "Just thanks for coming over, that's all."

"Part of the job," he answered negligently, and lit the last candle. The corner of the room was now lit with the soft warm glow of half a dozen candles, banishing shadows to the recesses. "There you go."

He turned to leave the room, and Kendra said quickly, almost too anxiously, "Are you leaving now?"

"Actually, I'd like to wait until the rain dies down a little, if you don't mind. It was hell driving over here."

"Oh." Her relief was immeasurable, but she hid it well. "Of course, I don't mind. It's the least I can do."

She wished she could read the meaning behind his smile, but he was standing in the shadows. "How about something to drink?"

"Warm milk?" she inquired without much enthusiasm.

"I think I can do better than that."

When he was gone, Kendra tucked her legs underneath her on the sofa and pulled down the ruffle of her nightgown to cover her knees. She realized how scantily she was clad and wished she had put on a robe. The thin cotton nightgown barely covered her thighs, the low scooped neck and tiny puffed sleeves were nothing if not revealing. Maybe he wouldn't notice in the dim light.

He returned with a snifter of brandy for her and a coffee cup for himself. "Wonderful," she exclaimed as she inhaled the rich fragrance of the liqueur. She glanced at him over the rim of the snifter. "You're not having any?"

"You need to relax; I need to stay awake for the drive home." He sank into the chair opposite her and lifted his cup. "Cheers."

A crash of thunder was accompanied by Maurice suddenly leaping from nowhere and landing on Kendra's lap. Kendra jumped involuntarily and gasped, almost spilling her drink. To cover her embarrassment she took a quick gulp of brandy and gasped again. Her eyes watered, and her ears roared. "Wow," she hoarsely, staring at the snifter with new respect. "I don't usually drink this stuff straight."

"It's meant to be sipped," Michael advised, amused.

"I'll remember that." She pushed Maurice away as he began to knead her thigh with his claws. Thunder rattled the windowpanes, and she shuddered. "I hate thunderstorms. They're so noisy. And mice. They're so creepy. And squirrels have no business inside a person's house. You know what else I'm afraid of? Winter. Isn't that stupid? Like I'm going to freeze to death in one of the most modern cities of America or get snowbound and run out of food. But I hate it when it starts getting cold. I guess it's because I can't control the elements." She glanced at Michael over the rim of her glass. "I'm babbling. You should stop me."

"Why? You keep on gulping that brandy, and I'll have all your secrets before the night is out. Come here, cat." He extended his fingers to Maurice, who was once again trying to shred Kendra's nightgown with his claws, and the cat turned his head attentively. After a moment he sprang down from the sofa and onto the arm of Michael's chair, where he settled down contentedly to have his ears scratched.

"I think he likes you better than he likes me," Kendra commented.

"I'm just the hand that feeds him."

The rain increased with a sudden deafening roar, and Kendra glanced anxiously at the ceiling. "You don't think the roof with collapse, do you? I mean, all that water getting under the shingles, rotting the wood—"

"It's just a small leak," he assured her. "You wouldn't even notice it in an ordinary rainstorm. Tell me some more secrets. What about your family?"

She was so grateful for the distraction from her immediate worries that she didn't even question the personal turn of the conversation. "No secrets there." She took another careful sip of the brandy. "It's just me and my mom. My father walked out on us when I was ten. He was a jerk.''

Michael nodded sympathetically. ''That's a delicate age for something like that to happen.''

''It sure is. As if a preadolescent girl didn't have enough to worry about. But as it happened it all worked out for the best. I learned at an early age the only person I could depend on was myself, and there was never any question that I would get a job and be self-supporting. It kind of gave me a head start on women's liberation.''

''Is that why you never married? Because of your father?''

In the candlelight Michael's eyes were gently curious and nonjudgmental, inviting confidence. Everything about him invited confidence: his voice, his easy, relaxed expression, his reassuring presence close beside her while the storm raged outside.

She regarded him thoughtfully for a moment, then answered slowly, ''No. I think if I could ever find a man who was stronger than I am or smarter than I am . . . I might consider it.''

A crease of amusement appeared in his cheek as he glanced into his coffee cup. ''Ah, now,'' he said softly, ''there's a challenge if I ever heard one.''

Her pulses speeded with his smile, and she quickly took another sip of brandy. ''Anyway, how did you know I've never been married? I didn't tell you.''

''Research,'' he assured her with a wink, and lifted his coffee cup.

Kendra wondered if that kind of research was standard fare or if it had a more personal meaning. Wondering caused a pleasantly confusing tingling sensation in the back of her throat, and she quickly turned her gaze back to her brandy glass. "Besides," she added, "as it happens, no one ever asked me."

"Because you never let anyone get close enough."

She glanced at him, startled into a defensiveness that suggested perhaps *he* was getting too close. But his expression was placid and relaxed, his eyes warm with the light of a dozen candles, and suddenly she understood. She sipped her brandy complacently.

"I know what you're doing," she told him. "You're trying to take my mind off my troubles by getting me to talk about things that are none of your business and—" she glanced up at him, a smile curving her lips "—that's nice. And don't tell me it's part of your job, because this is far above and beyond the call of duty."

"My job is to give you what you need," he answered easily. "And right now you need someone to sit and talk to on a dark and stormy night. Nothing complicated about that."

She wasn't sure she believed him, or perhaps it was that she didn't want to believe him. "Always the professional," she murmured. And she couldn't resist teasing him, just a little. "So why aren't we talking about furniture or menus or bathtub rings?"

"Because those *are* your problems," he responded promptly. "Besides, they're boring. I'd rather hear some more of your secrets."

"I'm not sure I want to tell you any," she answered with a touch of primness in her tone. "It doesn't pay to get too close to the staff, you know."

His eyes twinkled in the candlelight. "Think of me as a trusted family member or a priest. You can tell me anything. So," he invited, lifting his coffee cup, "how's your sex life?"

She pretended to give that serious thought. "Disappointing," she said at last. "Don't you think so?"

Only a slight twitch of his eyebrow betrayed amusement as he murmured, "I'm sure I wouldn't know."

"No, in general," she insisted earnestly. "All that anticipation, the incredible excitement, the promises in the dark, and then it's over. A lot of wasted energy for a few minutes of pleasure. Disappointing."

There was a speculative gleam in his eye as he replied, "My, you are just full of challenges tonight, aren't you?"

That made her nervous—or perhaps the reaction was merely a treacherous excitement—and she decided it might be wise not to pursue the matter even in jest. She tucked her nightgown more securely over her knees and added, "I was speaking in general, of course."

"You were also," he pointed out, "speaking about relationships, not just sex. Very revealing."

She definitely didn't like the way he said that, but before she could reply he leaned forward to place his coffee cup on the table and invited casually, "How would you like to go away for the weekend?"

The sophistication she had feigned only moments ago vanished in an instant, and she stared at him, stammering, "Y-you mean you and me? Alone—together?"

A slow appreciative grin lit his eyes. "If I weren't so afraid of *disappointment*—" he emphasized the word slightly "—I'd let you think about that for a minute. As it is, however, I think I'll save us both the embarrassment and assure you that it's purely a business trip."

She blinked. "Business? What kind of business?"

"I thought we could drive to the mountains and stay over in one of those little towns that are so famous for their antiques. Your partner mentioned you used to like to shop up there, and there are still lots of things you need for the house. The painters and carpenters are coming next weekend anyway, so it would be a perfect time for you to get away. I'm volunteering my services as driver, advisor and all-around work-horse."

Perfectly logical, impeccably thought out and all-business, as always. Was it disappointment she felt, or reluctance? She replied uncertainly, "Well, I don't—"

She was interrupted by an earsplitting crash of thunder and a flare of lightning that illuminated the entire room. Even before the thunder died away there was a sharp creaking and groaning, and the house was jolted by a shattering crash.

The brandy glass splintered on the floor as Kendra leapt to her feet with a cry, Maurice streaked across the room and Michael hurried toward the window. "It was a tree!" Kendra cried. "A tree fell on my roof!"

"Sure sounded like it," Michael said grimly, peering out the window. "I can't tell anything from here."

He came back to her, took her shoulders, and guided her back to her seat. "Sit down, you're going to cut your feet. I'll go outside and check."

Kendra heard the front door open and close on the storm, and she buried her face in her knees and moaned out loud. Was there no end to this? One disaster after another sought her out like an arrow after a bull's-eye and there was nothing she could do to stop it—nothing. It should have been comical, but Kendra didn't feel like laughing. She didn't know how much more of this she could take.

Endless moments passed while she sat huddled on the sofa and Michael braved the storm outside for her sake. She was just about to follow him, regardless of her bare feet and the broken glass, when she heard the door open again.

She looked at him anxiously as he shook the water from his hair. "It's just a limb," he assured her. "It doesn't look like it did much damage. I'll have the men take care of it tomorrow when they fix the roof."

Kendra buried her face in her knees again with a muffled sound that could have been relief or dismay.

Michael was beside her quickly, his warm arm about her shoulders, his voice soft with concern. "Hey, what's this? The independent woman is crying over a little thing like a broken limb? I don't believe it."

She lifted her face to him and was ashamed of the mistiness that burned her eyes. "Crying," she admitted thickly, "or laughing. I don't know which. Oh, Michael, why does everything always have to happen at once? Why can't life be *easy*?"

"Because it's just not, that's all," he replied soothingly. "Here. Come here." He applied a gentle pressure to her upraised knees, straightening them, and drew her close in the circle of his arm. "Stop acting like a hysterical woman, and I'll tell you a secret."

"I am not a hysterical woman!" But her assertion lacked some of the indignation she would have liked, because a sudden thrill of awareness had gone through her at finding herself in his arms. His chest was broad and strong, and when she rested her cheek against it, she could hear his heartbeat. He smelled of rainwater and soft laundered fabric, and it felt good to lie against him like this. Warm and secure and . . . good.

She moved her face against his chest to look up at him. "What's your secret?" she demanded after a moment.

"The answer to your question from the other night. Why I took this job."

She sniffed ungraciously and settled more comfortably against him. "I thought it was because I was so helpless and incompetent."

"And . . ." He touched her chin with his finger, tilting her face upward. The smile in his eyes flowed through her like honey and warmed her all over. "Because you have the biggest eyes I've ever seen. And the cutest nose." His eyes crinkled as he ran his finger down the bridge of her nose to the tip. "And I like the way you wear your hair. Because I couldn't stop thinking about you even when I was away from you, and every time I thought about you, I smiled."

Kendra's breath was caught in her throat and would go no further; she couldn't take her eyes away from his. Every part of her was glowing with awareness, suspended in uncertainty. She whispered, "That's— not very professional."

"Neither is this." And slowly, deliberately, he lowered his mouth to hers.

It was a tender kiss, sweet and gentle and undemanding. But from the first instant of contact something opened within Kendra, a rush of heat filled her veins and strength left her muscles. Nerve endings tingled and flared to life, and her head roared; she seemed to melt into him. She hadn't been prepared for this. Never had she expected anything like this.

Even when the kiss ended she still felt a part of it, heated with it, dazed by it. Her fingers were twined into his shirt as though for support, but she felt weightless, disconnected from everything except Michael. She opened her eyes and had a hazy vision of his face, flushed and damp and very near to hers. She could taste him; his scent filled her senses. She whispered, "You make me dizzy."

His smile was vague and his fingertips stroked her face. Electricity sparked from his touch, bringing every cell to life. "Is that bad?"

"I—I'm not sure. I think so."

"I won't do it again, then."

His lips nuzzled her neck as his fingers drifted lower, pushing aside the sleeve of her nightgown to bare her shoulder. A kiss followed his touch, fire on her naked skin. Kendra caught her breath sharply, helplessly. "I—maybe I was wrong..."

His lips sought hers again, and the passion that had barely begun before gathered force, swelled and took on a life of its own, leaving them helpless in the wake of its power. Michael's hand closed around her waist, massaging her skin through the thin material, then tightening and holding her as he pressed her close. Her lips parted to the invasion of his tongue, his heat, his taste, his texture filling her and mingling with her, infusing all her senses.

Her breasts were crushed against the thunder of his heart, and it seemed to have the same rhythm as her own; a single long rushing roar. She couldn't think, she couldn't breathe; she could only feel, and every moment was a new starburst of sensation as his hand traveled downward over the shape of her hip and her thigh and closed around her bare knee and then moved upward again. She clung to him, she opened herself to him, every fiber of her being ached for him. And then slowly, unwillingly, the kiss ended.

She could feel his breath on her hot cheek, and it was as unsteady as her own. His face was a blur but his eyes were a beacon, dark and bright and filled with life. She focused on them, unable to speak or move or do anything except cling to him and wait for the helplessness to pass.

His hand was unsteady as it touched her face and then drifted to her throat. His eyes followed the movement, and her skin seemed to cry out with pleasure from his touch.

He said hoarsely, "Kendra . . . I'm going home."

He moved away from her, and the absence of contact was like a physical ache. But she was helpless to stop him. She was helpless to do anything except search his face and whisper, "Why?"

He smiled, but the effort seemed to pain him. "Ask yourself that question again at nine o'clock in the morning in the bright light of day." The smile faded, and his voice dropped to a husky timbre as he added, "God knows I will."

"Michael. . . ." But that was all she could say. *Michael.*

He leaned forward and placed a light lingering kiss on the top of her head. "Good night, Kendra," he said softly.

And just like that, he was gone.

Seven

Kendra knew she was making a mistake. After all the mistakes she had made in her life, one would think that by now she would have learned to listen to her intuition. So why was she sitting in Michael's van on her way to the mountains for the weekend?

Since the night of the storm she had seen very little of Michael, and their few encounters had been brief and businesslike. He never, by word or gesture, referred to what had happened between them that night nor indicated that anything about their relationship had changed at all. After a brief bout with uncertainty and confusion, Kendra decided that she was relieved.

After all, nothing *had* substantially changed between them. And what had really happened that night? There she had been, a little tipsy on brandy, surrounded by candlelight and clad in only a thin nightgown; there he had been, strong and calm and reassuringly masculine. They were only human, after all. The attraction had been there from the first, she couldn't deny that, and if she were brutally honest with herself she had to admit that she had done nothing to discourage it. She could hardly accuse *him* of improper behavior.

All it amounted to, she assured herself, was one friend comforting another on a stormy night, and there was nothing wrong with that. In fact, she should be grateful for it. Why was she so nervous?

The answer to that was quite simple. Because she remembered what his kiss had done to her—she lay awake at night, remembering—and there had been nothing friendly about it. She should never have agreed to come with him this weekend. She was getting in over her head.

Then why was she here? Perhaps it had something to do with the mild challenge in Michael's eyes when he reminded her of the weekend plans and the realization that, if she refused, he would think she was afraid to be alone with him. She certainly could be as mature about this thing as he was, and the last thing she wanted was for him to think she attached more significance to the incident than he did. Or perhaps—and this was what really disturbed her—she was here simply because, somewhere deep inside, she wanted to be.

The first hundred miles or so had passed in relative ease as they discussed mundanities: the accommodations Michael had arranged, the purchases she needed to make, the work that was proceeding on the house in her absence. But when harmless conversation was exhausted Michael put a tape of Baroque music in the player to cover the awkward silence, and the past hour had been very uncomfortable indeed. Kendra tried to concentrate on the passing scenery, but repeatedly her attention kept straying to Michael—the way the wind from the open window tossed his hair, the little lines that formed around his eyes as he narrowed them against the sun, the way his hand negligently guided the wheel. He was wearing jeans and a chambray jacket with the sleeves pushed up; his shirt was open at the throat. He looked casual, relaxed and sexier than he ever had before.

Michael glanced at her and almost caught her staring. "Don't you like the music?" he inquired.

"What?" Kendra pretended to be roused from a fascinating survey of the scenery. "No, it's fine. Why?"

"You were fidgeting."

Kendra pushed at the rim of her sunglasses, tucked one foot beneath her, changed her mind and sat straight, caught herself fidgeting and deliberately stopped. "I guess I'm just not used to sitting so long. Is it much further?"

"About twenty minutes." He glanced in the side-view mirror and signaled a lane change. "Do you know what I've always liked about you?" he added casually. "You always say exactly what's on your mind. So let's not start playing games at this late date. What's bothering you?"

Kendra glanced at him uneasily, but knew if she didn't answer he would only prod and probe until some or all of the embarrassing truth was revealed. Feeling somewhat safe behind her dark glasses, she turned in her seat to face him and said, "To tell the truth, I'm wondering what I'm doing here. I don't usually do this sort of thing, you know—just leave town for the weekend with a—" she almost said "man," "—stranger, to do absolutely nothing but—"

"Have fun?" he suggested.

"Well, yes." A frown of annoyance came into her voice. "I've got work piled up on my desk and a cat to feed, and I don't really like the idea of all those workmen in and out of my house while I'm away..."

"One of my staff will be on hand at all times to supervise," he reminded her. "What else?"

She shrugged uncomfortably. "It's just ridiculous, that's all. You don't need me along, you could have done this all yourself, and I could be at the office working where I belong. I mean, wasn't that the whole idea? Leave all the details in your big strong capable hands while I concentrate on my work?"

"Everyone needs a break now and then," was his mild reply. "And if it makes you feel any better, think of this as work. Now, what's really bothering you? Are you afraid I'm going to make a pass at you?"

A muscle tightened in her chest; her pulses leapt with surprise. But she kept her gaze steady behind the protection of the glasses, and her tone was as casual as his when she inquired, "Are you?"

He checked the traffic in the rear-view mirror. "I don't make passes; they're juvenile. When I want a woman, she generally knows it."

That was hardly better than no answer at all, but probably more than Kendra wanted to hear. She turned to stare out the window again.

He glanced at her with a quirk of a smile. "Come on," he persuaded. "Ease up. Relax, have fun. You used to enjoy this sort of thing. You told me so yourself."

"I also told you I only enjoyed doing it for profit," she reminded him. "There's nothing fun at all about doing it for myself."

"Will you explain to me again why you have such a phobia about decorating your own house?"

"It's not a phobia," she insisted, "it's just not my style. I don't like owning things, collecting things, being tied down by *things*. It's stupid."

He nodded soberly. "The more you have, the more you have to lose," he suggested.

"Well . . . yes," she agreed, although she had the feeling he was reading more into her sentiments than she had intended. "And it's just not worth the time and energy."

"So," he said thoughtfully, "you only invest your energy in the things you can count on—your work and yourself. Relationships can end, so you're not interested in those. Possessions can be lost, so why waste time collecting them. An interesting philosophy. But a rather lonely one, I would think."

Kendra shifted uncomfortably in her seat, not liking the turn of the conversation. "I don't believe I ever said any of that," she pointed out with a frown. "And I don't like to be analyzed."

"I'm not analyzing," he answered, still in a rather distracted tone, "just trying to understand. You're a fascinating puzzle, Kendra Phillips," he murmured, "and I'm just beginning to put together the pieces."

There was something very disturbing about the way he said that, and Kendra did not ask what kind of picture he was beginning to form from the puzzle. She wasn't at all sure she wanted to know.

The inn Michael had selected was on a cul-de-sac at the end of a tree-lined street, a long low rambling structure with gingerbread trim and wraparound verandas, as quaint and as picturesque as anything designed from Kendra's imagination. She took off her sunglasses as she got out of the van, surveying her surroundings appreciatively. "Now this," she murmured, "is really nice."

Her eyes were busy as she and Michael went up the wide front steps and into the foyer, noticing every detail of the authentically restored turn-of-the-century home. The claw-footed coat rack by the door, the tall plant stand with its graceful Boston fern, even the tintype portraits in carved wood frames that hung on the walls—all of it exuded character and charm, and she was impressed.

The parlor, which now served as a reception area, was to the left of the foyer, a small, cozily cluttered room that was brimming with antiques and antique reproductions. "Oh, my," Kendra exclaimed softly to Michael. "This is wonderful."

"And look." He nodded toward the far wall. "There's your clock."

Michael moved toward the neat, middle-aged lady who sat behind the reception desk, and Kendra wandered off to explore the room. Many of the items were tagged for sale, which took something away from the air of authenticity, but none of Kendra's fascination was lost because of them. And the clock to which Michael had first directed her attention was so handsome that she was almost afraid to look at it too closely.

It was a beautifully carved cherry-wood grandfather clock, with double brass pendulums and an intricately etched glass-paneled front. It was exactly what she had had in mind when she had drawn the design for her foyer, and in such excellent condition that, until she found the craftsman's mark, she thought it must be a reproduction. But no, it was a genuine antique, and when she looked more closely she noticed that the numbers on the clockface were somewhat faded and that it kept less than perfect time—fifteen minutes fast by her watch. Those imperfections, she decided contentedly, only gave it character. She ran her hands lightly over the smooth wood, somewhat awed by the presence of something so old, so…permanent. She was afraid she was falling in love.

She walked over to the desk just as Michael was retrieving his credit card and the room keys—two of them, she noticed. He tucked both into his pocket, and she said, "You are going to send me the bill for all this, aren't you?" Until this moment, she had not even wondered how the finances for this trip would be managed. Michael had taken care of everything.

He glanced at her dryly. "I'll write myself a check the first chance I get."

Kendra turned her attention to the woman at the desk. "Could you tell me about that clock over there?"

The woman smiled. "It's beautiful, isn't it? It was built in San Francisco in 1893. I suppose some people would consider it a museum piece, but I've always thought what it really needs is a good home—you know, an atmosphere of family and stability around it. It still keeps time…" And she laughed as the clock began to chime the half-hour—fifteen minutes early. "Though not very accurately anymore, I'm afraid."

Eighteen ninety-three. That was almost a hundred years ago. Kendra had never in her life owned anything that old, or wanted to. What had gotten into her?

She opened her purse. "I'll take it."

"Wonderful." The woman beamed and went around the desk to check the price.

Kendra looked up from a futile search through her purse in chagrin. "Michael, I forgot my checkbook!"

Michael reached into his pocket and calmly brought out her flower-covered checkbook.

"I'll take care of the shipping and delivery," Michael told Kendra when the transaction was completed. "And you'd better give me that receipt, before you lose it."

Kendra passed the receipt to him, still somewhat stunned by her own impulsiveness. "A hundred years old," she murmured, shaking her head in disbelief. "What in the world do I want with something that's a hundred years old?"

He cocked his head toward her and looped his arm lightly around her shoulders as they started up the stairs toward their rooms. "Maybe," he suggested, "to remind you that some things do last forever?"

A frown of concern puckered her brow, and she glanced back over her shoulder. "I just got carried away. I can't believe I did that. Maybe I should—"

He laughed and squeezed her shoulders, a playful spark dancing in his eyes. "Are you having fun yet?" he demanded.

The warmth in his eyes seeped through her and made her lips tighten with a smile. His arm around her shoulders was easy and companionable, and the tension that had stood between them all week seemed to evaporate in that simple shared moment. The smile widened to a grin, and she heard herself admitting, "Yeah. I think I am." And for the first time in a very long while, she really was.

Kendra barely had time to appreciate the old-fashioned charm of her room with its sprigged chintz draperies and eyelet-covered tester bed, though the atmosphere was, like everything else about this place, perfect. She and Michael had arranged to meet for dinner in half an hour, for dining was early in the small mountain town and both of them were hungry. She showered quickly and changed into a bright blue flowered skirt with a wide elasticized waistband and a deep flounced hem, which she paired with a peasant blouse of a lighter blue. She slipped on a pair of sandals, snatched up a light shawl against the cool mountain evening and met Michael downstairs precisely on time.

His eyes smiled when he saw her, and that made her feel a glow inside, just as it always did. "You look nice," he told her.

"Thank you," she returned, allowing him to drape the shawl over her shoulders. "So do you. However," she felt compelled to point out, "you realize that the purpose of this trip was shopping, and all the shops are closed now. We should have waited and left in the morning. This is a whole night wasted."

"I was ready to leave at noon," he reminded her. "You're the one who had to stay at the office. Besides," he added, as he escorted her through the door, "the night is only wasted if you let it be."

She wondered what he meant by that, and wondering caused a treacherous little thrill to tingle in the pit of her stomach.

The restaurant Michael had chosen was within walking distance and, he assured her, offered excellent food and an acceptable atmosphere. He had left nothing to chance. Kendra could not remember how long it had been since she had been treated to an evening of carefree entertainment without having to do so much as even make the dinner reservations. It was a luxurious feeling to be able to simply relax and enjoy herself and let him take care of everything.

The restaurant was indeed charming, with dark pine paneling, a huge stone fireplace and exhibits of antique cookware and farm implements decorating the walls. The lighting was low and romantic, and Kendra smiled as Michael pulled out a chair for her.

"What?" he inquired, picking up on her amusement.

"I was just thinking." She glanced at him a bit coyly. "This feels like a date."

He assumed a grave expression. "Shall I ask for separate tables?"

"Separate checks will do," she responded demurely, and he gave her a reproving look.

Kendra's mood only improved as she looked at the menu. She ordered a thick steak with all the trimmings and was surprised when Michael made no comment relative to her diet. She felt positively triumphant when she ordered extra dressing on her salad and she could see him struggling to keep silent. But when she began to douse her potato with salt, he had apparently reached his limit.

"That's very bad for you, you know," he said disapprovingly.

Kendra made a face at him. "I know, I know. It will make me retain water and raise my blood pressure and lead to an early heart attack."

"So why do you do it?"

She shrugged. "I do a lot of things that are bad for me. I eat the wrong foods, buy the wrong house, pick the wrong lovers. It's like a habit. And you know what?" She liberally ladled sour cream onto her potato. "I like it that way. I'd be just fine if you and Patty and everyone else would stop trying to improve me."

"I'm not trying to improve you," he corrected, "just broaden your horizons a little. And—" he frowned as she added an extra dash of salt to her steak "—guard your health."

She gave him a look filled with exaggerated tolerance. "So what are you, a doctor in your spare time?"

"No," he admitted with a grin that almost could have been apologetic. "My brother is, though. And I guess after all those nights of helping him cram for exams I do know more about medicine than is good for me."

"Or anyone else," she added. But that was the first time he had ever referred to anything about his family or his background, and she was intrigued. "Do you have a large family?"

He cut into his chicken. "Three brothers, all younger."

"Funny," she mused. "I always pictured you as having sisters. Mean older sisters who were always pushing you around, and so now you get your revenge on the entire female sex by bossing *us* around."

"I don't boss people around," he corrected. "I merely guide them in the right direction. And I'm not looking for revenge on the female sex. I happen to like females, as a matter of fact. A lot."

"Well now, that's reassuring," she murmured, and his eyes twinkled.

She concentrated for a moment on her steak, and then she asked, "What were you before you were a house husband?"

"I was a headhunter."

She lifted an eyebrow. "Why doesn't that surprise me?"

"Corporate management," he explained. "I would assess the needs on a management level and then find executives to meet them."

"I know what a headhunter does." She took up her knife again. "It just seems like a strange transition to me."

"Not really. I just took the same techniques and applied them to a different market."

"And a more lucrative one," she suggested.

"Not necessarily. But definitely more satisfying."

"Why aren't you married?" she asked unexpectedly.

His expression was mildly reproving. "There you go with the personal questions again."

"I know. And you're answering them."

He seemed slightly surprised. "So I am." He took a sip of his wine and answered after a moment, "None of my staff is married. It's too distracting to deal with other people's problems when you've got the same sort of thing waiting for you at home."

"That doesn't answer my question."

He smiled. "Why should I get married? My work is my family—literally. I get all of the satisfaction with none of the commitment."

"The best of both worlds," she suggested thoughtfully.

"In a way," he agreed. "I'm content." And a very brief shadow of introspection crossed his eyes as he added, "most of the time."

She wondered about the times when he wasn't content and if those times came in the dark hours of the night when he lay alone in bed and who he thought of then. She determinedly made herself stop wondering and asked instead, "How did you learn to do all this stuff—cooking and cleaning and whatnot?"

He grinned. "My mom, who else? She used to say two things, 'Brush your teeth,' and 'Do you call that *clean*?'"

Kendra laughed. "Well, I'll bet she's proud of the way her son turned out now!"

His smile was gentle and reflective. "She would be," he agreed. "She died when I was fifteen."

"Oh." Kendra was chagrined. "I'm sorry."

"It was tough for a while," he admitted. "We were a close family—still are. It was a shock when we lost the most important part of it, but we all pulled together and took care of each other. Of course, since I was the oldest most of the taking care of was left to me. So if I'm a little bossy sometimes," he conceded with a slight tilt of his head, "I guess that's why. I've had lots of practice."

She thought about him at fifteen, alone and grieving yet stepping in to take the responsibility for three younger brothers. She thought about herself and the way she had felt when her father left, and a softness began in her, a slow uncertain reaching out to him that was the beginning of a tenuous bond. She smiled at him, and he smiled back. For a moment they shared something tender and undefinable; something very special.

She said softly, "You really enjoy your work, don't you? I mean, it's more than just a job to you."

"It's what I am," he answered simply.

She looked at him, so gentle, so earnest, so wonderfully uncomplicated, and she thought, *If you're not careful, Kendra Phillips, you could fall in love with this man.* And a faraway little voice echoed, *Too late. You already have.*

Quickly she turned her attention back to her plate, but not quickly enough. Michael caught her flustered look, and his eyes crinkled with a smile as he cocked his head toward her. "What are you thinking?"

She glanced at him. She felt warm inside—warm and happy and tantalized with the excitement of a wonderful discovery. Her lips drew up in a smile. "I was just thinking what a good time I'm having. I guess it wasn't such a stupid idea, after all, coming here."

He grinned. "I thought you'd see it my way. I must admit, you look a lot happier than you did on the way up here."

She shrugged and picked up her fork. "That's just because I'm having dinner. Food always makes me happy. And," she told him defiantly, "I intend to order dessert."

He flung up a hand in self-defense. "I didn't say a word. As long as your eyes keep sparkling that way, you can order the whole bakery. Dinner's on me."

She laughed, simply because it felt good to laugh and because she liked the way the lights in his eyes leapt and played in response. And she was happy.

Eight

They took the long route back to the inn, and Michael held her hand. The mountain night was cool, but Kendra was still warm inside, and she didn't have to look far for the reason why. It was good, being with Michael. She always felt good when she was with him—sometimes angry, sometimes exasperated, sometimes exhilarated, but always *good*; alive and warm and cared for.

Michael was always there for her, he always knew what she needed, he always thought of only the best for her. How many women were lucky enough to have a man like that in their lives? How easy it was to forget that this was only a job to him, how tempting to fall into the simple pleasure of his presence, for he was as irresistible as ever.

Kendra did not have the excuse of too much brandy and a frightening storm tonight; just being with Michael was an intoxicant. He touched her, and her skin glowed, he smiled at her, and excitement bubbled inside. She glanced at him, and she remembered the power of his kiss; remembering caused her stomach to tighten and her throat to go dry. *You are not going to do this thing, Kendra,* she told herself firmly. *You're not going to talk yourself into more trouble than you've already got, you're not going to get carried away, you're not going to fall in love with this man.*

There was nothing but business between them, she reminded herself. Business and—something inside her softened with the realization—perhaps the beginnings of a tenuous but beautiful friendship. That was good, it was real, and she was not going to spoil it all by inviting complications neither of them wanted. Just keep it simple.

Their arms were around each other's waists as they reached the inn and climbed the stairs to their rooms. It was an easy, natural gesture, and it felt right. *Simple,* Kendra reminded herself. *Thank you for a lovely evening; good night, see you in the morning. You are not going to invite him in. You are not going to make love with Michael Drake.*

And with that resolve firmly in mind, Kendra unlocked her door, turned to say good-night and kissed Michael softly on the lips.

The embers of passion caught and flared, instantly, inevitably and powerfully. No more than a touch, a breath, and Kendra's blood rushed, her senses spiraled. It was a soft gentle merging that swiftly gathered force and left her weak, disoriented, yearning.

When Kendra lifted her arms to encircle his neck, Michael gently caught her wrists, and it was he who pulled away first. She felt the unsteadiness of his breath on her cheek and the pounding of his heart against her hand. Slowly he lifted his face and looked at her.

His skin was glazed with a faint dampness, and his eyes were lit by an inner fire—yet dark with uncertainty and regret. And even through the clamoring of her pulses, through the daze of yearning and confusion that assaulted her and made her weak, Kendra knew rejection when she saw it.

A rush of humiliation burned her skin and plucked at her throat. She extricated her wrists from his gentle clasp and quickly stepped back over the threshold, forcing a smile that was bright and false. "Sorry, I forgot." Her voice was hoarse, and she hated the sound of it. "That's not part of the service. Good night."

She started to close the door, but he caught the edge. His expression was sober. "Kendra, we need to talk, and I don't think it's the kind of conversation we want to have standing in the hallway. May I come in?"

After a moment she stepped away from the door.

Kendra heard him close the door softly behind him, but she was walking across the room, her back to him, her hands clasped tightly before her and her head held high. "You don't have to say anything." She spoke to the opposite wall, her voice high and tight. Misery had lodged in her chest and left her breathless, so that her words sounded clipped. "I know. I'm a lonely woman who hasn't had a lover in a long time and you just happened to be there. I took advantage of you. I apologize. You can go now."

She heard his soft slow release of breath, but she did not turn to look at him. Nothing could have made her

look at him at that moment. "It's a bit more complicated than that."

"More complicated. I know." She tried to draw a
deep breath and almost choked on it. She stared
fixedly at the rose-and-blue-chintz pattern of the
wallpaper. "I don't want to do this," she said firmly.
"Why are you making me do this?"

"Kendra...." He said nothing more, just that single sad word that held volumes of unspoken thoughts
and fell empty in the room.

Kendra's muscles tightened as humiliation, frustration and confusion twisted with the residue of passion within her and made her stomach ache. "Do you
think I haven't been listening to you all these weeks?"
she demanded, pacing once across the narrow length
of the room. "You think I haven't seen what's been
happening—what you do so well, what you do for
dozens of women, hundreds.... My life is a mess, and
you straighten it out, so I start to depend on you.
You're always there, taking care of all my needs, and
I start to like it. Pretty soon I start wanting more, I
start being sucked in. I forget this is just a job to you
and start believing your publicity—the perfect husband in every way. Very neat. Very clever. Congratu-
lations."

His voice was low and strained. "Kendra, that's not
fair."

"Oh, I'm not blaming you!" She walked over to the
window and released the ties that held back the draperies. They fell closed like heavy wings, sealing out
the rest of the world—echoing like a caress in her ears.

She lifted her hand as though to smooth a fold of
the draperies but found herself clutching it instead, as
though in a physical effort to push back the anger and

the frustration. She tried to make her voice calm. "You warned me. And if there's one thing I'm not, it's gullible. I did my best. I fought you every step of the way, I told you to leave me alone, I did everything I knew how to keep from falling in love with you." Her muscles clenched involuntarily against the admission. She had not meant to say that, but now that the words were out there was no taking them back.

She heard his soft intake of breath. "Are you in love with me, Kendra?"

She turned, pain and helplessness swelling up inside her and making themselves known in her face and her voice. "I don't know!"

He came across the room to her, and her heartbeat measured every step. She wanted to back away, to raise her hand to ward him off, to turn her back on him in a firm and final dismissal. She did nothing.

His hands took her arms lightly, and she did not twist away. He held her with more than a physical grasp, more even than the hypnotic power of his nearness. He held her with her own helpless hope, a need whose strength she had not even fully recognized until he was near and holding her.

"First of all," he said quietly, "this hasn't happened with dozens of women or hundreds or even one other single woman in my entire life." His expression was controlled, and she could feel the tautness in the muscles of his arms, despite the lightness of his clasp. His voice, low and deliberate, rolled through her like a melody. "If one of my employees were to do what I'm thinking about now, I'd have him fired and probably arrested. I want you to understand that, Kendra."

"Always the professional." She couldn't keep the bitterness out of her voice nor the hurt from taking the form of anger as she challenged him. "Well let me tell you something, *Mr.* Drake. There's been more than one time when you acted a little less than *professionally* and you're not going to stand there like a perfect innocent and make me feel guilty for coming on to you. It's not fair!"

He dropped his eyes briefly. "No, it's not," he admitted huskily. His thumb made an absent, stroking gesture against the sensitive flesh of her forearm, causing her skin to prickle. "It's hard to act professional when all I can think about is making love to you whenever I'm around you. You make me forget what I'm supposed to be and how I'm supposed to act. Sometimes I try too hard not to forget, and then I make you angry. Sometimes I don't try hard enough and—" Nothing but a soft breath and the smallest resigned lift to his shoulders finished the sentence.

Kendra's breath was suspended, every muscle in her body poised in expectation as he lifted his eyes to hers again. "I made a mistake, Kendra," he said quietly. "I knew from the beginning what you could do to me, and I never should have taken this job. Oh, I've tried to rationalize it in a thousand ways, but the fact remains it was wrong to agree to this arrangement when I knew from the first moment I saw you how easy it would be to fall in love with you."

Hope flared, bright and joyous, and then died with his next words.

"Kendra, please try to understand." His hands tightened briefly on her arms. "You are the most special thing that has ever happened to me. But this can't go on. I've just got too much to lose."

A swift hot bolt of shock and outrage went through her, and she jerked her arms away, staring at him. "Your job?" she exclaimed incredulously. "Are you talking to me about your *job*?"

His face flushed, and his lips compressed with anger, but Kendra backed away from him, flinging accusations as quickly as they burst up within her. "That's it, isn't it? Your precious professional reputation!" Her voice grew more shrill with every word, and his eyes grew darker. "Are you afraid I'll report you to the house husbands' union? Sue you if you're not good in bed? Well, let me assure you, Mr. Drake—"

"Kendra, stop it!"

The explosion startled her into silence; the raw emotion in his eyes swallowed up her petty anger and made her feel small. "You know it's not just the damn job! I wish to God it were that simple."

He took an angry step toward her and then stopped himself with a curt, controlled gesture. He half turned from her as he ran his hand through his hair, and when he looked back his eyes were churning and the muscles in his jaw were taut. The hurt and fury that radiated from him was like a storm held barely in check, and the power of it took her breath away.

"Damn it, this isn't a game to me," he said tightly. "I can't afford to be just another one of your 'wrong lovers,' another item on your list of mistakes. And—" he released a soft, frustrated breath "—I know you too well to ever think I could be anything else."

His last words held a note of weariness and defeat that sobered Kendra more than his anger could. *He's right,* she thought. *Let it go. This is all wrong, it will never work out and you'll be much happier if you just let it go.*

But she wrapped her arms around herself in an instinctive gesture of self-defense, and she met his gaze with a stubbornness too long ingrained to be abandoned now. Her voice was high and sharp as she retorted, "You always know best, don't you? What's good for me, what I want, what I need. Well, why don't you let *me* decide what I need for a change?"

He spread his hands in a brief gesture of exasperation. "Then *tell* me!" he demanded. "Tell me, if you can, because I don't think you know! You want to be independent, so you hire me to run your life. You want to take care of yourself, but you won't even learn to balance your own checkbook. You tell me to stay out of your personal life in one breath, and in the next you're melting in my arms. Tell me, Kendra," he demanded, "what do you *want*?"

"I don't know!" she shouted back. Her color was high, and her fists were clenched. She knew in her mind that everything he said was reasonable and right, but none of it mattered. All that mattered was what she was feeling, and what she was feeling had nothing to do with logic. "I don't know anything anymore! Everything used to be so simple until you came into my life. I used to know what I wanted, I had everything I needed." Her short, indrawn breath had a choked sound, and she looked at him helplessly. "But now—now I feel like I don't have anything, and I just don't *know* anymore!"

"Oh, Kendra." The words were like a sigh, and he closed his eyes slowly. When he opened them again, there was such tenderness and regret within them that she felt her chest constrict as though in an instinctive movement to protect her heart.

"Don't you see?" he said gently. "You said it yourself tonight. I've built a life-style out of avoiding commitment, of having the best of two worlds, of giving on my own terms and never getting involved. Yes, I like my work, and yes, it's more than work to me, but the most important part has always been that I can walk away at the end of the contract, don't you understand that? And with you . . . I can't walk away. Because loving you, taking this thing between us even one step further is going to jeopardize more than my professional integrity. It will mean rearranging the way I think and the way I've lived and the things I've thought were important. It would mean forever."

How strong he looked standing there, within arm's reach, the lamplight glinting on his dark hair, his harsh, lean face softened with sincerity. How strong, and how vulnerable. How badly she wanted to touch him, and how desperately she determined not to.

Kendra's throat was swollen and her breath was tight. The next words were barely a whisper. "I'm not asking you for forever."

He looked at her sadly. "I know. And that's exactly why you're too big a risk for me to take."

Too big a risk. Of all the things he had said to her, all the things that were battering at her and swirling and darting in her mind, this stood out the strongest. Michael was afraid. Michael, who was always so calm and confident, who knew the place for everything and kept everything in its place. Michael, who never had a doubt nor a moment's hesitation, was just as afraid of commitment as she was. He wasn't perfect.

A soft, faintly rueful smile touched her lips, though she did not feel like smiling at all. "How strange," she murmured. "All those lectures you gave me about growing up and taking responsibility, and deep down inside you're just as insecure as I am. That's kind of funny. We match."

He looked away from her. "Too well in some ways," he agreed quietly. "And not enough in others."

She raised her chin, her eyes narrowing. She said simply, "I may not be perfect, Michael Drake, but neither are you. And if nothing else, I'm glad I found that out."

He turned back to her, sorrow and reluctance evident on his face. "Kendra, I don't want to hurt you— God knows I don't want to hurt myself. I'm just trying to make this easier."

And that was too much. "Easier!" she exclaimed. She made a terse, impatient gesture with her wrist as the tension within her escalated to the breaking point. "You're always trying to make things easier! Well, you may know everything there is to know about cooking and housekeeping and budgets and cats, but you *don't* know everything about me! Maybe we'd both be better off if you just took care of your personal problems and your professional integrity and stopped trying to make things so *easy* all the time!"

He was quiet for a moment, studying her in a way she couldn't read and wasn't sure she wanted to. His gaze made her flush, or perhaps it was only the accumulated embarrassment of the past moments, and she had to look away.

"I guess some things are never easy, are they?"

She felt a twinge of pain, a sharp regret for all she had lost and was about to lose, and she swallowed hard against it. "No," she said briefly and without looking at him. "I guess not. And now—" she made herself raise her eyes to him "—if you'll excuse me, I think my dignity has taken enough of a beating for one evening and..." She gestured vaguely toward the door. "Maybe you'd better just go."

The light in his eyes was deep and intense, and he looked as though he might say something else. Expectation and need leapt within Kendra, and she squelched them deliberately, turning away. Why was she torturing herself? It was better this way.

She heard his footsteps cross the room, and she focused blindly on the chintz pattern of the wallpaper, tightening her jaw against the bitter, confused emotions that assaulted her. *Par for the course, Kendra,* she thought. *Wrong time, wrong place, wrong everything.* But at least this time she had been spared the full consequences of a messy mistake. She should be grateful for that.

But she didn't feel grateful at all. And she wished Michael would hurry up and leave because she was very much afraid she was going to cry.

She heard a sound behind her, but it wasn't the door being opened. It was the soft click of the lock.

She turned, confusion and uncertainty scattering within her. Michael was leaning against the door. He watched her quietly, thoughtfully for a moment, and then he said simply, "I resign."

"What?" Her breath left her in a stunned and horrified gasp. "You—after all this—after all you put me through...you *what*?"

At that moment all she could think about was that he was leaving her, she would never see him again; she had wanted too much, and she had driven him away. He couldn't do this. She couldn't let him do this. How could he *do* this?

His expression was calm and composed, his tone mild. He said, "That's the first step, isn't it? To take our relationship off the professional level and give the personal side of it a chance to grow."

Her heart was beating hard, and she looked at him narrowly, half-suspecting some trick. "What are you talking about?"

A soft, barely visible smile etched his lips as he pushed away from the door. "I don't want to be your employee anymore, Kendra. I want to be your lover."

Her heart leapt to her throat and lodged there for a breath-stopping moment. She watched him move toward her, and everything within her seemed to form into a single, wondrous syllable, *Yes*.... But then hurt resurfaced, and anger, and she flung up a hand to ward him off. "Don't do me any favors!" she said shortly.

He shook his head with a soft chuckle that was resigned and amused. "Honey, if I were thinking about doing either one of us a favor, I'd be outside that door."

He continued to come toward her, and Kendra felt an immensely foolish urge to back away. Her face was hot, her fingertips tingling and her heartbeat was like a rapid whir of hummingbird wings loose in her chest.

She stiffened her muscles and stood her ground. "And what if I don't accept your resignation?"

"Then—" his head tilted slightly with a faint smile "—I'm afraid I'll be in serious violation of company policy."

He was less than three steps away from her now, so close that she could see the texture of his freshly shaven skin, smooth and bronze over his cheekbones and darker, coarser where the shadow of his beard began on his jawline. So close she could see the faint, almost imperceptible shadow that was cast upon his forehead by one errant lock of hair and trace the lines that radiated around his eyes. His scent tantalized her, drifted through her. She could almost feel his body warmth. She couldn't take her eyes away from his.

"What about..." Her voice sounded thick, and she swallowed. "What about the contract? The termination...penalty."

"You'll be reimbursed in full," he assured her, and his hands fell upon her shoulders, light, caressing, enveloping.

She inhaled for retort, an objection, a stinging phrase that would put him in his place and recompense for some of the misery he had put her through. But it was as though the very act of breathing closed the distance between them, drawing her into his arms, evaporating her will and melting her resistance.

She leaned against him, her arms creeping around his waist, her cheek resting against his chest. For a moment she was dizzy simply from the wonder of being near him, enfolded by him. She felt the deep expansion of his chest and the soft warmth of his sigh against her hair as his hands moved upward over her back and her bare neck, cupping her skull.

He said huskily, "This is the stupidest fight we've ever had. You know that, don't you?"

She whispered, "Yes." All her attention was focused on the quick, aching rhythm of her heartbeat and the slow strong counterbeat of his against her ear.

"Do you think we can maybe act like grown-ups now?"

His lips touched her neck, sending a shudder of hot liquid pleasure though her. Her hands slipped beneath his jacket, floating over the soft cotton material of his shirt and the lean muscular planes it covered. "You make me so angry," she murmured.

"You..." She felt his smile curve against her neck. "Charm me." His lips touched the lobe of her ear and brushed against her temple. "Enchant me." He pressed a light warm kiss against the hollow curve of her collarbone, and she caught her breath with the sensation. "You make me crazy."

She tilted her head up to look at him, her neck supported by the cradle of his hands. Her breath was a shallow, ineffectual thing that was almost completely lost in her need for him, a poised and poignant expectation that consumed her reason and left her weak. She searched his eyes, his face. She saw no secrets, but neither did she see answers. She did not want to ask the next question. "What changed your mind?"

"Nothing." His voice was sober, but his eyes were alight, quiet and certain. "My mind still tells me this is wrong." He took her hand and placed it lightly over the strong, steady thump of his heart. "But that's not what I'm listening to," he added softly.

A tenuous joy exploded inside Kendra and floated upward like bubbles in champagne. She looked at him, filling her senses with him, reveling in him. Nothing had ever felt so right. Nothing.

She reached up and touched the corner of his eye with an unsteady fingertip, tracing the curve of his cheekbone, brushing the feathery texture of his lashes. "You have pretty eyes," she said throatily.

Those eyes crinkled with a smile as he turned into her caress. "So do you."

He lowered his face; his mouth covered hers.

If ever there had been hesitation or uncertainty between them, there was no more. They came together in instinctive hunger and unshielded need, greedy and urgent. Kendra's lips parted, and his tongue entered, a slow thorough mating of taste and touch that sent surprised heat flooding through her veins, roaring in her head. His hands tightened on her waist, then in firm, possessive strokes moved downward to her hips, drawing her closer and cupping her against him. His thighs were rigid against hers, the muscles of his shoulders taut and straining with need. He was power and strength; he overwhelmed her and made her weak, he filled her and made her strong.

"Kendra..." Dimly she was aware of his husky whisper, of the brush of his lips across hers as he spoke. "You make colors explode inside my head."

She opened her eyes, and his face was a blur of warmth and passion, of adoration and need. She lifted her hands and threaded them through his hair, letting it fall like strands of fire through her fingertips. She wanted to caress all of him like that, to gather him close by handfuls, memorizing and exploring, luxuriating in the wonder of him.

"I lied before," she whispered.

The tip of his tongue lightly traced the shape of her lips, his breath drying the moisture there. "About what?"

Kendra's breath was thready from his caress, and her reason no more steady. She wanted to melt into him. To just close her eyes and lose herself in him. "I do know what I want." Her breath stopped completely as he pressed a kiss to her throat and then resumed shakily. "I want...you. Just you. Loving me."

"That's all I've ever wanted. If you will just...let it be."

His mouth covered hers again, and again ecstasy spiraled, sweeping her away in a haze of sound and color. She could drown in his kiss, could happily die while wrapped in his arms. Except that when she was in his arms she was more alive, more vital and energized and aware than she had ever been before, and kissing him was like tasting immortality.

His hands moved downward over her ribs, slowly, agonizingly. His thumbs brushed her breasts, tracing their shape through the soft fabric of her blouse, and tight electric bolts of awareness burst from his caress, robbing her breath and catching in her throat. His fingers moved downward to her waist, slipping beneath the wide elastic band of her skirt, drawing the material downward as he caressed her buttocks and her naked thighs below the panty line. Every nerve, every cell, every pore of her body opened to him, absorbing his touch, aching and yearning for more of him.

The skirt billowed around her ankles, and Michael's hands came up, cupping her face. He looked at her so deeply, so intensely, that she thought her heart would stop from nothing more than the soul-absorbing power of his gaze. The bed was two steps away.

He removed his clothes quickly, without order or care, then he sat upon the edge of the bed and just looked at her for a long moment. He was naked, she was not, but the heat of his gaze made her feel as though their positions were reversed; she was anxious and taut with anticipation, and his eyes burned her skin.

She lifted an unsteady hand to his arm, caressing the smooth shape of his biceps. He was lean like that all over. Lean and bronze and perfect. She whispered, "You make me tremble, just looking at me."

His smile was slow and gentle, it began in his eyes and spread leisurely, almost absently, to his lips. His voice was husky. "You make me weak, just looking at you."

His hand cupped her face, stroking it, moving downward to her throat. She turned her face to his hand, inhaling deeply of his scent and released the breath in a sigh. "This feels so right."

"Yes...."

He took the hem of her shirt and the chemise beneath it, and tugged them over her head. Hardly had she felt the touch of the cool room air on her bare breasts before his hands warmed her, his mouth dipping to caress and taste, electrifying her nerve endings and sending tight ropes of need from her throat to the core of her abdomen. She writhed against the sensation, against the urgency; her hands closed on his waist and felt smooth taut flesh and damp heat. She flattened her palms against his back as a gasp of pleasure escaped her, and she traced the shape of his body with her hands and with her legs, pressing into him, memorizing him by taste and touch, absorbing him.

He hooked one thumb beneath the lace edge of her panties and slowly slipped them over her hips. His hand traced a light silky pattern upward on the inside of her thigh, and his touch left starbursts of pleasure in its wake. She thrust her fingers into his hair, luxuriating in the satiny feel of it as it floated through her fingers, urging his face to hers. She entwined her leg with his, seeking his mouth. She tasted salt on his face, rubbed her cheek against the slight coarseness of his jaw, inhaled his hot unsteady breath. She felt his mouth upon hers, blending in moisture and heat and certain need. And easily, simply, as naturally as drawing breath, he was inside her.

It was a slow sweet filling that seemed to take forever as every thought, every breath, every need was suspended, caught in rapture upon the sensation. And then he was deep within her, so deep he was more than a part of her. He was still, holding her, pressing her to him, letting the moment swell between them, filling them, sealing them together. Kendra closed her eyes tightly, and she thought, *So perfect. So right. How could I not have known?*

For she hadn't known. She had recognized need, yes, and she had sought to fulfill it blindly, instinctively, like a child who knows only that she *wants* without considering the consequences of her desires. But until this moment she had not known the power of her need nor the depth of its fulfillment. For there was more than physical pleasure in this simple act of joining they shared. There was discovery, there was wonder, there was even a little fear. In that single moment they were no longer two, but one, and slowly, inexorably, Kendra felt a space open in her life that could never be filled by anyone but him.

They melded together perfectly, their bodies drawing from each other the instinctive rhythms of life that were as old as time but as new as the next moment. They moved with slow, smooth sensual strokes, each sensation treasured and savored, each moment captured as an entity unto itself. His flesh, strong and slippery beneath her hands, her muscles straining, his breath whispering across her face. The touch of his lips, the caress of his hand, so light, so adoring, on her forehead. And when she opened her eyes there was his face, flushed and damp and soft with pleasure, his eyes deep and alight and focused on her, only her. She thought, *Forever. This could last forever. Oh, Michael, why didn't you tell me?*

But urgency built, their movements became more demanding as wonder gave way to need. Kendra felt sensation expand and blossom, then focus sharply into a pinpoint of desire that was Michael, who was all her world. Only Michael. His thrusts were deeper and more powerful, and she rose to meet him, crying out his name in one last explosive burst of sensation that seemed to release her from herself and make her a part of him. Forever, a part of him.

For a long time she lay dazed and quiescent in his arms. Her muscles were stripped and toneless, her skin still tingling, the pace of her heartbeat and her breathing scattered. Swirls of light danced behind her closed eyelids, and she floated with him, safe in the circle of Michael's embrace. She could hear his breathing, soft and unsteady, against her ear. His fingers were light on her throat, moving gently in a soothing hypnotic caress.

She wanted to wrap her arms and legs around him and hold him tightly. She wanted to make love to him again, and again, all through the night. She wanted to simply lie here with him, in stillness and wonder, forever.

Darts of exhilaration took her back to what they had shared, and would share again, then faded into quivers of joy that were followed by a pervasive peace. But the contentment was mixed with equal measures of surprise and uncertainty. For she had never expected to feel so moved, so changed, so deeply rearranged inside. She had never expected making love with Michael to be this...important. Her own feelings confused her and disturbed her a little.

Michael shifted his weight, bending over her with a smile. Playfully he brushed a damp strand of hair away from her forehead. "*Now* are you having fun?" he demanded.

She laughed, and the laughter wiped away her foolish concerns. It was only Michael, whose smile made her feel light inside, who could take away all her cares with a word, who balanced her world on the tip of his finger.

She wrapped her arm around his shoulders and pressed her face against his chest, breathing deeply of the warm, damp male scent of him. "Oh, Michael," she murmured. "Why did we wait so long?"

He touched a kiss to the top of her head. His voice was husky and indulgent. "It hasn't been long."

"It feels like a lifetime." With the words, the full significance of all she had missed and all she had just found washed over her and left her weak. Once again uncertainties prickled as the vastness of the future spread before her, but she pushed them back determinedly, tightening her embrace. "*My* lifetime," she added in a whisper touched with awe. "My whole lifetime...waiting for you."

And then she looked up at him. "Is this as difficult for you as it is for me?"

"What's that?"

"Being this happy."

He smiled, absently and tenderly separating strands of her hair with his fingertips. "Even harder. You have this incredible ability to just wade hip-deep into life and field whatever comes along. I, on the other hand, like things a bit more orderly. I guess I think too much."

The smallest touch of anxiety tightened her throat as she searched his face. "What are you thinking now?"

He bent and placed a long, lingering kiss on her forehead. "Just how much I love you," he answered softly.

Kendra released a sigh and settled into his arms, secure in the knowledge that, for tonight, that was enough. More than enough.

Nine

The next day they went shopping, and Kendra made purchases with a happy abandon she had not imagined was possible. Perhaps it had begun with the grandfather clock or perhaps it had something to do with Michael, but she was no longer just decorating a house—she was building a home. Each selection was thoughtfully debated and lovingly chosen, and every piece had a place in her heart long before it took its place in her house. She bought china napkin rings and hand-painted porcelain candlesticks, a mirror in an antique gold-leaf frame and a small brocaded chaise for the foyer that only needed refinishing and re-upholstering and would be as good as new. The highlight of the day was the discovery of a stereoptiscope in a dusty, little-frequented junk shop, and Kendra was able to haggle the owner into a more-than-reasonable price.

"I'm glad to see you got over your shopping phobia," Michael commented dryly as he made room for yet another carefully wrapped package in the overcrowded van, and Kendra laughed. It was true: she had never suspected before how satisfying, how expansive and *permanent* the simple act of furnishing her own home could be. For the first time she felt sorry for her own clients, who would never know the joy, the sense of belonging, that came with knowing that a little part of oneself was going into even the most trivial decorative item in the home.

Or perhaps it was the fact that, when she envisioned her finished house, she also imagined Michael sharing it with her, and that was when it really became a home.

One of their last stops of the day was in a little curio shop. It was the kind of place that catered to tourists with uncertain taste and unlimited budgets, and Kendra did not really expect to find anything there. She wandered around, frowning over price tags and giving cursory attention to an occasional china doll or Hummel figurine, until a display of music boxes caught her eye.

A reminiscent smile touched her face as she picked up one of the ceramic boxes. It was cheap and touristy, with two statuettes on top dressed in eighteenth-century garb posed in the steps of the minuet. "I had one of these when I was a kid," she murmured, examining it. "Only mine had a ballerina on top."

"What happened to it?" Michael inquired.

She shrugged. "Who knows? I never have been able to hold on to anything for long." Her expression softened as she remembered. "I really loved that music box, though. After my dad left, I used to wind it up and just sit and watch the ballerina go around and around for hours, and I could forget, for a while, how bad things really were.''

She wound up the music box and then laughed with delight as the two figures on top began to twirl with the tinny sound of the ''Emperor Waltz.'' ''My favorite waltz!'' she exclaimed.

Michael's eyes grew soft with the pleasure he saw reflected in hers. ''Why don't you get it?'' he suggested.

''What would I do with it? It's not even in period. It won't go with the house.''

''But you like it.''

''It's silly and tacky. The figures are dressed in eighteenth-century clothes and dancing to a nineteenth-century waltz.''

''You couldn't buy it for sentimental reasons?''

''I'm not a sentimental person,'' she responded lightly, and put the music box back on the shelf. But she couldn't prevent one brief, very sentimental glance backward as they left the shop.

Michael left her browsing in a crystal and silver shop as he went to bring the van around, and by the time he returned she had bought two vases and a silver tea service. ''A *tea* service,'' she murmured with a wondering shake of her head as Michael found a place for the latest purchases in the van. ''Imagine me with a silver tea service. Who do I think I'm going to serve tea to in this day and age?''

Michael grinned and squeezed her shoulders. ''Me,'' he informed her with light kiss on her cheek. ''In bed.''

She laughed, glowing with his brief caress and with the vision his words induced. "That's your job!" she returned pertly.

He winked at her. "Not any more."

By the time all of the packages were removed to Kendra's room for safekeeping, there was hardly space left over to walk. Kendra sat on the bed, which was the only available sitting area, and looked around in dismay. "I can't believe I bought so much! How are we ever going to get it back in the van? Do you think it will all even fit in my house?"

Michael picked his way carefully around bundles and sacks and sat beside her, surveying the situation thoughtfully. "You don't have much room to move around in here, do you? Maybe you'd better move into my room for the night."

Her eyes twinkled mischievously. "Why, sir! Is that a proposition?"

"Not at all," he assured her, straight-faced. "I'll sleep in here. I don't need as much space as you do."

She struck out at him playfully, and he wrestled her to the bed, laughing. With her head resting against the pillows and her hands caught lightly in both of his, she looked up at him, breathless from more than exertion. His eyes were sparkling and his face was flushed, and her legs were captured between his, and as they looked at each other playfulness faded into tenderness, a new and richer kind of excitement.

Kendra said softly, "Let's make love."

"All right." He lowered his lips to hers, clasping them gently. "But first..." He released her hands and sat up. "Don't get mad at me."

Kendra struggled to a sitting position, watching suspiciously as he began to search through the pile of boxes on the bedside table. "What have you done?"

He found a small white box and presented it to her. Curiously, Kendra pulled aside the tape and lifted the lid. The music box was nestled inside.

For a moment she couldn't speak. Her throat felt thick and her eyes prickled with moisture as she lifted the box out of its wrappings. She turned the key, and the room was filled with the tinkle of the waltz.

"Everyone deserves to be silly and sentimental sometimes," Michael explained.

She looked at him, and such a swell of tenderness and adoration filled her that she thought she would cry from the sheer beauty of the emotion. With the music box still held in her hand, she wrapped her arms around Michael's neck. "I do love you, Michael," she whispered.

His arms tightened around her in a gentle, thorough embrace that only began to touch the depths of what they were each feeling for the other. "I am so glad," he said, and his own voice was husky. "Because the feeling is very mutual."

He took the music box from her and placed it on the table, and he lowered her again to the pillows. They made love with slow exquisite languor in the dying rays of the afternoon sun, and afterward they lay together in sweet and perfect silence, wrapped in the wonder of all they had discovered and begun to share over the past two days.

Two days. Tomorrow they would leave, and the idyll had been far too short. Kendra did not want to go back to work, to the daily frantic routine and the roles each of them had grown accustomed to playing in the other's life. She wanted to stay like this forever.

After a long time she asked softly, "Michael... what will happen when we go home?"

His hand, which had been cupping her shoulder, lifted to trace a light caressing pattern on the side of her face. It was a soothing gesture, kind and reassuring. "What do you want to happen?"

Kendra closed her eyes, a smile of pleasure softening her lips. "I want... you. I want to go to the movies with you, and out to dinner, and I want to spend long evenings at home with you watching television or talking and afterwards I want to go to bed with you and know that you'll be there when I wake up in the morning. I want to make love with you. A lot. I think..." And she looked at him, a little hesitantly. "I want you to live with me."

He smiled. "No, you don't."

Almost, hurt prickled. Only the gentle, amused look in his eyes forestalled it. "Why not?"

"Because I'd drive you crazy. You'd feel crowded and nervous and start looking for reasons to fight. Our relationship isn't ready for that kind of strain, Kendra. Trust me."

She tried to accept that in the spirit it was meant, mostly because she suspected he was right. It would be difficult for her to learn to share her life with a man, and it would take time. But for the first time in her life she was willing to try. Eventually she would be ready... and so would he.

"But," he added, tweaking a strand of her hair. "I will take you to the movies, and out to dinner."

She glanced askance at him. "Will you still cook for me?"

"As often as you cook for me."

She muffled a groan. "You don't know what you're asking."

"All right," he decided quickly, "I'll do the cooking."

She chuckled and then sobered. She turned her head to look at him again. "You didn't answer my question," she reminded him. "What do you think is going to happen when we get home?"

There was no levity in his expression now, and she thought she even saw a touch of sadness in his eyes. "Honey, I know what's going to happen. And there's not a thing in the world I can do about it."

For a moment her breath stopped. She searched his face anxiously. "What?"

He leaned forward and kissed her forehead. "You're going to break my heart."

She relaxed, because she thought he was teasing. She shook her head adamantly against the pillow. "No, I won't."

"It's a sure thing."

"Shall we make that a bet?"

"Consider it done." His hand stroked her thigh, his forehead rested lightly against hers as his body moved over hers again. With a sigh of pleasure, she lifted her arms, welcoming him. But there was bleakness behind the tender smile in his eyes as he added softly, "This is one bet I hope I lose."

There was a certain strangeness to the sensation of coming home with Michael, of mounting the steps hand-in-hand with him, turning her key in the lock while he waited with her bags. She was a different woman from the one she had been when she left two days ago. Michael was a different man to her than he had been when he first strode through her door, assessing weaknesses and planning strategy like a military commander. There was no denying the fact: *everything* was different now. She just wasn't entirely certain which forms the differences would take. And that uncertainty, quite predictably, made her anxious.

But the uneasiness that was just beginning to gather in the back of her mind vanished the minute she stepped into the foyer. "Michael!" she gasped. "My clock!"

She ran to it, touched the polished case and ran her fingers lightly over the etched scrollwork on the glass panel, hardly trusting her eyes. "How did you get it here so quickly? I didn't know you were going to...Michael it's my clock!" She turned to him, delight coloring her face and shining in her eyes.

He gave a casual lift of his shoulder, but his pleasure in her reaction was obvious. "A few extra dollars tacked on to your shopping bill was all it took. They delivered it yesterday. It looks good in here, doesn't it?"

She looked back at the clock, studying it with growing appreciation and wonder. The addition of the clock transformed the foyer from an empty, useless space to a statement of elegance and permanence. It was perfect, it was exactly what the room needed, it was hers. She laughed out loud, barely able to restrain herself from clapping her hands with childlike enthusiasm. "Yes!" she exclaimed. "It's wonderful. It looks like...why, it looks like it belongs here."

"It does," he reminded her. "It's yours."

He set her bags at the foot of the stairs, and there
was a secretive anticipation in his eyes as he took her
arm. "Come on. Let's check out the rest of the place."

She was so distracted with her pleasure over the
clock that she barely wondered what he meant until he
stopped at the entrance to the living room.

"Oh...my." Kendra brought her hands to her
cheeks, and the two words were all she could manage
as she stood there, surveying the miracle that had been
wrought in her house.

Sunlight streamed over a cherry rolltop desk and
formed abstract patterns on a delicately colored Au-
busson carpet. A cluster of petit-point chairs and di-
vans was drawn up before the fireplace, a polished
wood butler's cart awaited her tea service. Pie tables
and fern stands were arranged at artful angles, covered tables and shadowboxes stood ready for her collection of knickknacks. A reproduction armoire
concealed her entertainment center on one wall; a
graceful camelback sofa seemed to be made for snug-
gling. As perfect as a picture, Maurice was curled up
on a hassock in a patch of sunshine; he looked up
sleepily as they came in, then resumed his nap.

"It's my room," she said softly, and took a few
steps inside. From the fringed and prismed lamps and
the tasseled cushions to the pale peach tint of the walls
it was, detail for detail, exactly as she had extracted it
from her imagination. She had lived so long with this
particular design in the back of her mind that seeing
it transformed into reality did not seem strange at all—
it was simply comfortable and familiar, like coming
home.

"It perfect," she said wonderingly. "Just perfect."

"Not quite," Michael pointed out. "It still needs those personal touches only you can give. All those things you bought in the mountains cluttering up the place. Just don't forget to dust them."

She laughed and flung her arms around him. "Oh, Michael, *this* is why you wanted to get me away this weekend!"

"I know you said you wanted to do it in small doses," he admitted, "but I couldn't stand the suspense. Now come on." He slipped his arm around her waist and urged her from the room, no longer making an effort to conceal his enthusiasm. "Let's see the rest of it."

It was like walking through a fairy tale or the corridors of her own favorite daydream. The library, with its Persian carpet and heavy wine-leather furnishings; the Oriental elegance of the dining room with its black lacquer table and chairs and painted screens. The earthy, inviting atmosphere of the kitchen, complete with copper pots and woven baskets. But it was the solarium that most took her breath away.

It was an ethereal forest of hanging plants and fragrant blossoms. Airy white wicker furniture was arranged beneath lush green trees, hidden alcoves shaded marble benches and delicate statuary. The air was thick and moist, the atmosphere lush and still. And set up in one corner, an anachronism captured in a brilliant flood of light, was her drawing board.

"Oh, Michael."

For the longest time she could say nothing more. How could she thank him for what he had given her? He had brought into her life not only comfort and pleasure, but purpose, meaning, *roots*. He had made her fantasies reality and given her a reason for caring about them. He had given her more, even, than a home. He had given her a whole new life.

She lifted her arms to his neck, her fingertips curled around his shoulders, and let him read for himself the joy that was in her eyes. She saw it reflected back in his as he inquired softly, "Like it?"

"Oh, yes." Her fingers slipped down to the first button of his shirt and released it, then the next.

"You haven't even seen the bedroom yet," he reminded her.

"It can wait."

Pleasure leapt in his eyes as she released the final button of his shirt, and his voice sounded a little breathless as she pressed a long warm kiss against his chest. "Are you sure?"

"Positive."

She tugged at his belt buckle and released the snap of his jeans. She let her tongue trail over his abdomen and felt the muscles quiver there. He tasted like sunshine.

His fingers tightened on her shoulders as she tugged the zipper of his jeans downward. "This floor is cement," he commented hoarsely. "And cold."

"There's a chaise."

"It's narrow."

"We'll manage."

She lead him there, and together they fell to the soft cushion in a swift bold fever of tangled clothing and straining muscles, of muffled sounds and hot, urgent touches until Michael caught her face between his hands and whispered breathlessly, "Slow down."

"Why?" She was on fire for him, as she always was, but today more than ever. So much was bursting inside her, so much she wanted to share with him and give him, so much joy that was theirs only for the grasping.

He smiled and brought his face again to hers in a slow and lingering kiss. "Because," he murmured, "I want this to last for a long, long time."

And it did.

If there could be a single pat phrase to describe the following weeks it would be "almost perfect." Kendra could never have imagined what a difference would be made in her life by the simple presence of a home: a place to go to that was welcoming and pleasant and orderly, a place of comfort at the end of the day, a place that was alive with all that was uniquely her own. She never got tired of exploring the nooks and crannies in her new dwelling place, the subtle touches and dramatic surprises she had hardly been aware of incorporating in the design. She could spend hours admiring the cozy warmth of the living room or basking in the tropical splendor of the solarium. Every spare moment was happily filled expanding and refining her decorating scheme, for once the nesting instinct took hold it did not let go.

And then there was Michael. The afternoons with him at art galleries and bookstores, happily debating the merits of various pieces of art and literature and lovingly selecting each piece that was to find its way into her home. In the evenings they went out, and Michael was as entertaining and as attentive a companion as she ever could have wished. And the nights of tenderness and passion in his arms, discovering more about each other in silence than they could have with words.... It was more, much more, than Kendra had ever imagined.

This was not just a playful interlude or a beautifully intense love affair whose ending was already marked. Those things Kendra was accustomed to, and she knew how to deal with them. This relationship with Michael was something completely new to her, for it had from the beginning been underscored with permanence. He was the man she had looked for, waited for, all her life. He was every secret wish and daydream come true, and she loved him with an intensity that took her breath away. Perhaps that was what frightened her so. Or perhaps it was simply that it was all so... almost perfect.

"How can you say 'almost'?" Patty declared after her first thorough tour of the house. "This is fantastic! It's glorious! Look at this place—it's your dream house, and I've known you too long to listen to any halfhearted protests to the contrary. And look at yourself. You've finally got it together. You haven't missed an appointment or bounced a check in weeks, even your clothes match. You're in love, you're organized, you're so happy I have to dim the lights when you come into a room. You've got the perfect house, the perfect lover, the perfect housekeeper, the perfect *life*, and I'm so jealous I could strangle you. What can you possibly find to complain about now?"

Kendra smiled wanly as Patty sank into a deep velvet chair, kicked off her shoes and wriggled her toes luxuriously in the carpet. "He's not supposed to be working for me anymore," Kendra pointed out.

"So?" Patty reached for an apple from the silver fruit bowl at her elbow, biting into it contentedly.

"So," Kendra tried to explain, "*he's* the one who balances my checkbook and reminds me of appointments and makes sure the cupboards are full and that my laundry is done and my car is serviced. It's like a habit he can't break.''

"And you *object* to that?" Patty challenged incredulously.

Kendra frowned uncomfortably. "No, not really. I love it. I'm grateful. It's just that . . . he does so much for me and I never get to do anything for him. Or even for myself. I feel—" she flushed a little, knowing the words were ridiculous before she said them "—like a pet.''

Patty gave a choked bark of laughter and then went into a spasm of giggles that made her eyes water. She recovered herself and made a diligent effort to address Kendra's problem seriously.

"Then let me ask you this," she proposed. "If Michael didn't do all these things for you, who would? Let's just be brutally honest for a moment and think back to how this whole thing got started in the first place. Do you really think you're capable of running this house, doing your job, keeping your life in order and still having the energy left over to enjoy everything you've worked so hard to acquire?''

The question made Kendra uncomfortable, because there was no easy answer. "I don't know," she replied at last with a small, disturbed sigh. "I guess maybe what I'd really like is a chance to find out.''

That chance came sooner than she expected or even wanted.

Ten

You should give a party," Michael suggested casually a few nights later.

They were driving home from the Realtors' Association dinner at which Patty had been the guest speaker. Patty had been a smash, the dinner had actually been edible, and Kendra, with Michael on her arm, had been the envy of every woman there. There was a definite satisfaction in knowing that she was with the handsomest man in the room—and one of the few men in the world besides James Bond who could wear a white dinner jacket gracefully. It was wonderful to get all dressed up in her festive pouf-skirted white dress and know that Michael thought she was beautiful, and it was wonderful to feel his arm slide possessively about her bare shoulders when it became obvious other men thought so, too. It was positively exhilarating to go to one of these requisite affairs with a real date rather than someone she had dragged out of her Rolodex at the last minute. But there was so much more to it than that. With Michael she was comfortable. He could catch her eye at an inappropriate moment and make her giggle over a shared unspoken opinion about one person's speech or another's flamboyant mannerisms. He could touch her hand under the table and thrill her inside. He could smile at her and make her feel like the only woman in the room. When she was with him, she was part of a couple, and there was something both indescribably wonderful about that and a little frightening.

She glanced at him now in the passing glow of a streetlight and inquired, "Do you mean like a housewarming party?"

"Maybe." He made the turn onto her block. "Or a celebration party."

"What would I celebrate?"

"How about success?"

"You don't give a party just because you're successful. I've been successful for a long time, and I've never given a party for it. We need something more specific."

He thought for a moment. "What about an engagement party?"

She turned to him in genuine surprise. "Oh? Who's getting married?"

He pulled into her driveway, extinguished the headlights and switched off the ignition before turning to her. Still, she wasn't prepared when he answered simply, "Us."

She stared at him. The faint glow from the porch lights cast intriguing lines and shadows over his face, gently highlighted the ends of his hair and darkened his eyes to a soft, rich velvet green. Eyes that were patient and watchful, quietly waiting—and seeing, she was afraid, far too much behind the arrested expression in her own eyes.

Quickly she looked away, her hand traveling uncertainly to her throat as though the physical gesture could urge from it the response he wanted. But all she could manage was the parroted syllable, "Us?"

"That's right." Perhaps that was a smile she heard in his voice, perhaps she only wanted to hear it. She couldn't look at him.

"I—I don't understand." She wound her index finger through the pearls at her throat and then quickly made herself stop before she broke the string. "A little while ago you didn't even want to live with me."

"I don't like to do things halfway," he admitted.

Kendra managed a nervous laugh, but it sounded dry and very strained. "No. You never did."

She could feel his gaze upon her, tender and quiet and undemanding, and she could not say another word.

Why couldn't she answer him? Why wasn't she flinging herself into his arms and covering his face with kisses between breathless exclamations of "Yes!" She *loved* this man. Her life was only half complete without him, every aspect of her happiness revolved around him, he was a part of her in a way no one else could ever be. When people loved each other like that, they got married. They devoted themselves to each other, they joined their lives and their life-styles together, they promised to stay together forever. That was what she wanted, wasn't it—to be with Michael, forever? Then why couldn't she say the words?

Michael's arm rested across the seat. She felt his fingertips lightly stroking the back of her neck. His voice was sober and unsurprised, yet heart-breakingly gentle. "Still afraid of commitment, Kendra?"

His touch, so light, so silky, made her want to turn into his arms and never leave; the low, familiar timbre of his voice tugged at her heart. But inside something was tensing and resisting, and she answered a little stiffly, "Is this a test?"

His hand fell away, and she turned to him in swift chagrin. "Oh, Michael I didn't mean—" And then she broke off in helplessness and pleading. "Why?" she insisted. "Why are you doing this?"

She expected to see hurt in his eyes and hardness in his face. But instead she saw only sadness. "Maybe it was a test," he admitted. He dropped his gaze for a moment, and when he looked back at her his smile was weak and very false. "I warned you, didn't I, that with you it would be forever?"

"All or nothing," she whispered.

His smile was quiet and touched with regret. "I'm afraid so."

Then he opened his door and got out.

The few short steps up the walk were some of the most agonizing of Kendra's life. Thoughts and emotions raced and collided with one another; she knew she should say something but she didn't know what to say. How had her life gone from blissfully serene to achingly complicated in such a few short moments? What was *wrong* with her? Michael was the man she loved; the only man she had ever loved. Why couldn't she give him the answer he needed?

At the door he handed her keys to her, and she looked up at him anxiously. "You're not coming in?"

He shook his head. "Not tonight," he answered quietly.

She inserted her key in the lock and noticed distractedly that it didn't click. She couldn't let Michael leave like this. They had to talk. She had to think. They couldn't leave this hanging between them.

She pushed opened the door and turned on the light. She started to turn back to Michael, but then stopped at the expression on his face. He was looking past her into the foyer, and he said softly, "Good God."

Kendra gasped as she followed his gaze. Her beautiful grandfather clock was overturned on its side, the glass panel shattered. Nothing remained of the landscape she had proudly hung on the foyer wall a week ago except the empty hooks. Someone had been in her house!

Michael swiftly grabbed her arm, but she broke away, her heart pounding in her chest as she ran toward the living room. What she saw there so stunned and sickened her that she could not even cry out.

Only the heaviest pieces of furniture remained. Magazines, books and papers were littered over the floor, artwork had been stripped from the walls, bric-a-brac overturned and crushed. The stereo, television and VCR had been torn from the entertainment center. The rolltop desk, the reproduction chairs, the antique tables, the stereoptiscope, even the carpet...all were gone. Nothing remained but the odds and ends of an empty shell.

Kendra screamed, *"Maurice!"* And rushed up the stairs.

She found Maurice under the bed, and she also found that her drawers had been ransacked, her jewelry stolen and her wallet—which she had carelessly left on her dresser when she changed to her evening purse—was gone. She came down the stairs with the cat cradled in her arms and tears of shock streaking her makeup. She didn't even feel the tears; all she felt was the nightmare.

"All of my things," she murmured, and her voice sounded high and distant, like a sleepwalker's. "They took all of my things...."

Michael's face was grim as he took her arm. "They did a thorough job," he said. "The silver, the china, the microwave—everything that wasn't nailed down. I guess with all the vans that have been coming and going lately the neighbors didn't notice anything unusual. I've called the police. They don't want you to touch anything else."

Kendra barely remembered the police coming or anything about the hours that followed at all. Michael took care of everything. She sat with Maurice on the heavy camelback sofa, one of the few items the thieves had apparently not considered worth the strain of removing. Every time she would notice some new item missing she would remember the moment she and Michael had purchased it, or the pride she had felt in designing it, and the ball of pain within her would expand until she thought she would choke from anger, hurt and loss.

When the officers told her they were leaving she did collect herself enough to inquire of one of them, "Will you—will you be able to get my things back?"

He looked at her sympathetically. "I'm sorry, ma'am. Not a chance. These were professionals."

When the police were gone the silence was eerie, the aftermath of devastation complete. Until then Kendra had let the disaster sink in by bits and pieces; now the entire picture spread before her, and it was almost overwhelming.

"Well," she said in a very small, very dull voice. "Easy come, easy go, huh?"

Michael sat beside her, his arm going around her shoulders in a tender, encouraging embrace. "Come on," he said gently. "You're coming home with me tonight."

Kendra leapt to her feet in sudden agitation, and Maurice sprang to the floor. "My credit cards!" she exclaimed, beginning to pace as she pressed her fingers to her face. "My driver's license, my social security card—my checkbook! I'll never get that all straightened out! I'll be weeks running all over town—"

"Don't worry about it," Michael soothed, getting to his feet and coming over to her. "I'll take care of it."

"All my things!" She spread her hands helplessly, indicating the ransacked room. "Michael, all those things I bought in the mountains, I picked them out, they were so perfect for this room.... My clock! Did you see what they did to my clock? It was an antique, it can't be fixed, not like it was—ever since 1893 and now...!" A broken breath cut off the words, and she couldn't go on.

Michael's hands fell lightly on her shoulders. "Honey, you're insured. It can be replaced, all of it. We'll just start over, that's all..."

"No!" She jerked away from him, her voice high and her face mottled with wild emotion. "No, it can't be replaced! It was *mine*, and now it's gone and it can't be replaced!"

Michael drew a hand through his hair and said softly, "Damn." He looked at her with sympathy and regret, and behind it all was a self-directed anger. "This is my fault. I should have had a security system installed. I knew you needed one. I should have insisted. None of this would have happened if I had taken care of it when I should have, but the first thing I'm going to do in the morning is get somebody out here. You're not spending another night in this house unprotected. Now, come on. Let's go home."

"No!" she shouted at him. She jerked her arm away as he reached for her, and he stopped, startled. "That's not your job! None of this—" she made a terse, angry gesture around the room "—is your job!"

Her face was hot, and she felt the sting of angry tears on her skin, but she scrubbed them away distractedly. "You *did* your job, okay, Michael? I never wanted any of this. You made me get these things, you made me care about them, and now they're gone and it's enough! I don't want to start over, I don't want to go through it all again. I just want to be *left alone*."

The words were harsh, and she knew she was hurting him; she saw the carefully controlled mask come over his features and she thought, *Michael, stop me, don't let me do this*. But he said nothing, and she could not stop herself.

Her eyes glittered, and her voice was tight as she cried, "Michael, don't you see? You can't protect me from everything. You can't make everything easy for me. You couldn't protect me from this, and there's nothing anyone can do, ever, to make it easy! I don't *want* you to protect me! I want to take care of myself, and if I don't do it very well then that's too bad, but at least I'll be *trying*!"

His face was very still, and the expression in his eyes was not denial or shock but a strange and reluctant sort of understanding that hurt Kendra more than it reassured her. She hated the words that she had just heard herself say, she hated the confused tumultuous emotions that prompted them, and inside she was crying out for him to do something, say something that would make it better. But she must have known all along that he could not, for everything she said was true. He couldn't protect her from this; he couldn't make it easier for her. There were some things she had to face on her own, and one of those things was the acceptance of who she was, deep down inside.

He said sadly, "How strange. One of the first things I loved about you was your free spirit, and that was the first thing I took from you. I thought I was helping you, but all along I was just making things easy on myself and making you dependent on me. I'm sorry, Kendra."

She gulped for air, and rubbed her aching throat. She thought, *No! That's not what you're supposed to say. You're supposed to tell me I'm wrong, you're supposed to tell me everything's going to be all right, that you'll take care of me. Michael, I don't want this to happen!*

But her own fear was more powerful than her needs, and the demon of hurt was battering her inside, taunting her and pushing her. *The more you have, the more you have to lose.* She had known better. From the beginning she had known better than to become attached, to take on more than she could handle. She could not keep holding on to things she was destined to lose. It hurt too much.

Kendra closed her eyes and took a short, choked breath that hurt her chest. "Michael," she said brokenly, pleading with him to stop her even as she spoke, "I love you, but I can't go home with you. I can't let you take over, I can't let you take care of this, and I can't..." The words almost would not come. She squared her shoulders and forced them. "I can't marry you. I just want my life back." Yes, her life back the way it was before everything was so easy and everything was so perfect. Before Michael.

A slow and solemn understanding came into his eyes and eventually made its way to his lips, where it traced a small sad smile. "All I ever wanted was to give you what you need," he said softly. "I guess the only thing you need from me now is your freedom."

The words twisted and squeezed at her heart, and she wanted to cry out against them. No, that was not what she wanted. Not freedom from him, not anything without him. But her fists clenched slowly at her sides, and the only words that would come were tight and choked. "I have to do this alone."

He came forward and stood before her, and she could feel everything that was real and precious within her shatter into a million irreplaceable pieces in that long moment that he looked at her. Then he leaned forward and kissed her lightly on the cheek. He said quietly, "Looks like I just won a bet."

And he turned to go, but at the door he looked back. In his eyes was too much understanding, too much sorrow...too much love. With absolutely no effort at all he read her tormented thoughts and said softly, "No, love, I'm not going to try to stop you. You've had too much interference from me as it is, and this time it has to be your choice. But just re-

member one thing—nobody can take anything from
you that you refuse to give up.''
     And then he left.

     A long time later Kendra went into the solarium—
the one room the thieves had not seen fit to disturb.
She sat down on the chaise, and Maurice leapt up beside her. She brushed him aside and pulled her knees
up to her chin. As he leapt onto the wicker table beside her, Maurice knocked something over. Her music box. The tinny little tune began to play, the
baroque figures turning awkwardly on their sides, and
Kendra started to weep. She couldn't stop for a long
time.

     For the next week Kendra's hours were occupied
with the mundanities of trying to put her life back together. Insurance forms, banks, police reports, the
thousand and one details that form the foundation of
a respectable, well-ordered life. The driver's license
bureau, the credit-card companies, hours on the
phone. Once she would have thrown up her hands in
exasperation and refused to deal with any of it. If Michael had been there she would not have been required to deal with it; all would have been taken care
of for her, quietly and efficiently. But now she took an
almost masochistic pleasure in tackling the bureau-
cracy and coming out ahead. It took her mind off
more pressing pains.
     When Patty expressed her horror and sympathy
over the break-in Kendra merely gave a callous shrug
and replied, ''You clutter up your life with a lot of
useless junk and you're just inviting thieves. So let
them have it. It's better this way. Simpler.''

And over and over again she repeated that reassurance to herself. It was better this way. She was back at square one, with nothing but herself and her work to worry about. She had always known it was a mistake to try to expand her life, to reach for more than she could grasp. She would be happier now. Just as she had been before.

Patty appeared to be taking the entire episode harder than Kendra was. Repeatedly she offered her own apartment for Kendra's use, and when she asked if Kendra wasn't afraid to stay in the house alone after what had happened, Kendra merely replied, "What's there to be afraid of? I've got nothing else to lose."

And that was the truth of it. Once she had had everything: a home, a fulfilling career, a love. Now she had nothing. She couldn't concentrate on her work; her designs were dull and uninspired. Her house was a cold shell to come home to, forbidding and empty. And Michael . . . Michael was everywhere, his smile filtering over her with the morning light, his voice echoing in empty halls, the ghost of his touch brushing over her in the soft still hours of the night. She thought it would get easier with time, but it didn't. And she was unhappier than she had ever been in her life.

Patty came into Kendra's office one morning to find her sitting at the drawing board, pen in hand, a blank sheet of paper before her. Kendra did not look around when Patty entered, and Patty cleared her throat hesitantly before she spoke. "Umm, excuse me. But you don't seem to have made a lot of progress since the last time I was in here—two hours ago. Is anything wrong?''

Kendra looked at her thoughtfully. ''I was just wondering . . . why do they do it?''

Patty came into the room hesitantly. ''Who?''

''Our clients.'' She made an absent gesture toward the blank paper. ''Why do they pay us to do this? We give them the perfect house from doorstop to doorbell, and they give us a great deal of money, but in the end they have nothing. Because it's not really theirs at all. It's ours.''

Patty gave a puzzled shrug. ''You know why as well as I do. They're not willing to invest the time or the energy to do it for themselves or they don't trust their own taste or they're afraid of making a mistake.''

Kendra slid down from the stool and walked slowly toward the window. ''Nothing worth having comes without risk,'' she murmured almost to herself. ''And if you're not willing to lose something, you're never going to have anything.''

She frowned, absently tugging on the necklace around her throat as she tried to put the elusive, nebulous thought into words. ''It's like . . . Michael and me,'' she said. Slowly it was becoming clear, a truth that had been waiting in the back of her mind fully formed for a long time but that she had been too reluctant—or frightened—to recognize. Now it was struggling into the light, and the power of it was slow and certain and wonderful in its simplicity. ''I hired Michael to make things easy for me, but nothing that's real is easy, is it? There's no such thing as a shortcut. When things start to get hard, that's when they matter the most.''

"Kendra," Patty said hesitantly, "I've tried not to get too deeply into this thing. After all, it was kind of my fault that you and Michael got together, and God knows I did more than my share of pushing you into this house business. I guess I feel kind of guilty. If I'd stayed out of it, you wouldn't be hurting now. But, Kendra—" she paused, uncertain, and then went on determinedly "—it's beginning to look to me as though the thieves took more than a few pieces of furniture and jewelry, things that are a lot more important than your credit cards and your microwave. Things like—like your faith in yourself and your willingness to try."

Kendra was silent for a long moment, then she said softly. "They can't take anything from me I refuse to give up."

She turned suddenly, a surge of triumph and determination bringing color to her cheeks and a sparkle to her eyes. "I'm giving a party," she announced, "this Friday."

Patty took a startled step backward. "*This* Friday?"

Kendra gave a decisive nod and strode toward her Rolodex to begin the guest list. "That's right. We'll invite all our clients and—"

"But—but that's crazy!" Patty stammered. Clearly she was afraid her friend had cracked under the stain. "My apartment's not big enough for all those people, and your house is a mess! You haven't replaced any of the furniture, and you told me yourself you only have two drinking glasses. You can't possibly get things in shape for a party by Friday!"

Kendra glanced up, her eyes sparkling with excitement. Even as a small, secret smile of confidence curved her lips. "Just watch me," she replied.

By eight-thirty Friday night the house was filled with the sound of clinking glasses and laughter. The caterers moved back and forth between the kitchen and the dining room, keeping the buffet table stocked with delicacies that happy guests devoured. Kendra received compliment after compliment on her innovative use of space and color and graciously declined to explain that the entire decor had been put together in less than a week. The living room was furnished with an electric mix of functional and decorative pieces that Kendra had selected on impulse and instinct from the warehouse floor; the dining room was chrome and glass for easy care, and the kitchen was hardly a gourmet haven. The walls were devoid of artwork and the decorative shelves were mostly bare, but the finishing touches would be added with time and love. No, it was not Victorian, and no, it was not complete—but it was uniquely her own.

Kendra stood in the center of the room, festively dressed in a strapless paisley hostess gown and dangling gold earrings—costume jewelry, because that was her style—and she tried to take pride in what she had accomplished. And she *was* pleased. She had done this all herself, and whatever else happened this would always be hers. But deep beneath her well-earned satisfaction there was an aching hollowness, and it was becoming harder and harder to keep her smile in place.

Patty squeezed through a cluster of people to stand beside her, her eyes shining. "I wouldn't have believed it!" she exclaimed. "Just look at this place—

you did it! It's a great party, Kendra, and the house looks, well, unbelievable! Who would have thought you had it in you?''

Kendra forced one more smile. "I guess you never know until you try." Then she dropped her gaze briefly to her drink. "He's not coming," she said softly.

The excitement in Patty's eyes faded to sympathy, and she patted Kendra's arm. "I'm sorry."

Kendra looked up and took a bracing breath, once again forcing brightness into her tone. "So, what's one party? I'm not giving up. I'll call him tomorrow and the next day and the day after that. I can be one stubborn person when my mind's made up, and that's something Michael Drake should have learned a long time ago."

"Maybe he already has," Patty said softly. She was looking beyond Kendra's shoulder, an Kendra turned quickly. Michael was making his way slowly through the crowd toward her.

With about two feet separating them and a dozen laughing chattering people surrounding them, Michael stopped. The voices, the shifting bodies, the sound and movement faded away for Kendra, and nothing remained except Michael. His lean bronze face filling her vision, his forest-green eyes gentled with a smile, the curve of his lips, the breadth of his shoulders. Michael. The anvillike stroke of her heart repeated the word, *Michael*. Her breath swelled inside her chest, happiness unwound within her. For a moment she couldn't speak. She couldn't do anything but look at him, absorb him.

Then he said simply, "Hi."

Her voice was breathy and uncertain as she replied, "Hi." A thousand words hung between the lines.

He glanced around briefly "I like the way you've done the house."

"It's not perfect."

His eyes returned to her. His smile lingered. "I know, that's what I like best about it."

Oh, Michael, Michael.... A dozen things, a hundred, clamored inside her, aching to be expressed but there were no words for any of them. People jostled and moved around them, but Kendra hardly noticed. She couldn't take her eyes off Michael. And his never left hers.

She said in a rush, "I wasn't sure you would come."

He answered gently, "I was just waiting for you to ask me."

Something tightened inside her chest and almost broke. Was it happiness or need? She said with difficulty, "I—said some awful things to you...that night."

"That's what I always loved about you, remember?" he reminded her. "You say what's on your mind. And what you said that night was the truth. I'm glad at least one of us could see it. A relationship shouldn't be built on dependency or need, even if it's with the best intentions. You had to find your own way. I'm glad you did."

Still the unspoken words echoed between them. The air was practically filled with them. She wanted to fling her arms around him, embrace him hard and cry out loud her love for him for everyone to hear. But instead she held his gaze and said determinedly, "I can't let you run my life, Michael. No matter how great the temptation is."

He nodded. "Fair enough. One of the things I've learned recently is that I seem to have enough trouble running my own life." A faint, rather rueful smile touched his lips. "Perhaps if I'd done a better job of that, you and I wouldn't be having this conversation now."

She searched his face anxiously. He wasn't reacting as she had expected, and nothing about his reaction gave her cause for encouragement. But she had to go on. This time they had to do it right. "I don't need you to take care of me. I have to take care of myself."

He smiled, and he reached forward and lightly clasped her fingers between his. "Maybe," he suggested gently, "we could take care of each other."

Lightness and wonder swelled inside her, leaving her weak, leaving her free. Her gaze was on his, and she saw love there. And promise. Her words were barely a breath. "Fair enough."

For the longest time they simply looked at each other, and the whole world faded away in the moments that were suspended between them, hovering on the edge of forever. Then someone jostled Michael's arms, pushing him closer to Kendra as he laughingly excused himself. Kendra's pulses leapt with the contact, and a light of pleasure kindled in Michael's eyes.

He glanced around, then back at her. "Nice party," he commented. "What are we celebrating?"

Kendra's throat was dry. She looked at him hesitantly. "An engagement."

His eyes were busy on hers, but his voice was mild. "Oh? Whose?"

She could barely form the word. "Ours?"

He smiled and lifted his hand to her face, lightly stroking her cheek, fingertips feathering against her hair. Her whole world was filled with him, and she saw the reflection of herself in his eyes. "In that case," he murmured, "may I kiss the bride?"

She whispered, "Please do."

And he did.

* * * * *

Silhouette Desire ®

1989
IS THE YEAR
OF THE MAN!

What makes a romance? A special man, of course, and Silhouette Desire celebrates that fact with *twelve* of them! From Mr. January to Mr. December, every month has a tribute to the Silhouette Desire hero—our **MAN OF THE MONTH!**

Sexy, macho, charming, irritating . . . irresistible! Nothing can stop these men from sweeping you away. Created by some of your favorite authors, each man is custom-made for pleasure—*reading* pleasure—so don't miss a single one.

Mr. January is Blake Donavan in RELUCTANT FATHER by Diana Palmer
Mr. February is Hank Branson in THE GENTLEMAN INSISTS by Joan Hohl
Mr. March is Carson Tanner in NIGHT OF THE HUNTER by Jennifer Greene
Mr. April is Slater McCall in A DANGEROUS KIND OF MAN by Naomi Horton
Mr. May is Luke Harmon in VENGEANCE IS MINE by Lucy Gordon
Mr. June is Quinn McNamara in IRRESISTIBLE by Annette Broadrick

And that's only the half of it—
so get out there and find your man!

Silhouette Desire's

MAN OF THE MONTH . . .

MOM-1

ATTRACTIVE, SPACE SAVING BOOK RACK

Display your most prized novels on this handsome and sturdy book rack. The hand-rubbed walnut finish will blend into your library decor with quiet elegance, providing a practical organizer for your favorite hard-or soft-covered books.

Only $9.95

Approximately 16" x 8" when assembled

Assembles in seconds!

To order, rush your name, address and zip code, along with a check or money order for $10.70* ($9.95 plus 75¢ postage and handling) payable to *Silhouette Books*.

Silhouette Books
Book Rack Offer
901 Fuhrmann Blvd.
P.O. Box 1396
Buffalo, NY 14269-1396

Offer not available in Canada.

BKR-2A

*New York and Iowa residents add appropriate sales tax.

Silhouette Desire ®

COMING NEXT MONTH

#481 NIGHT OF THE HUNTER—Jennifer Greene
Meet our March *Man of the Month*, Carson Tanner. Proud.
Elusive. He prized freedom above all else, but when he met
Charly Erickson, freedom never seemed lonelier.

#482 CHANCES ARE—Erica Spindler
Men were a challenge to unconventional Veronique Delacroix.
But when she decided to date her boss on a dare, she found the
stakes getting too high—even for her!

#483 THE ROOKIE PRINCESS—Janice Kaiser
Coach Nick Bartlett couldn't believe a woman the press had
dubbed the "Rookie Princess" was now his boss. But Hillary
James was nothing like he'd expected . . . and all he'd dreamed of.

#484 AS GOOD AS GOLD—Cathie Linz
From the moment smooth-talking attorney Bryce Stephenson
strode into her life accusing her of gold-digging, Susan Cantrell
sensed trouble. And Bryce was trouble—in more ways than one.

#485 WOMAN IN THE SHADOWS—Sara Chance
He appeared in *Southern Comfort*—now James Southerland is
back in a story of his own with Suzanne Frazier, an intriguing
woman playing a dangerous game of deception.

#486 BUTTERFLY—Jo Ann Algermissen
Handsome ex-rebel Seth Kimble returned home only to find
Vanessa Monarch caught in a gilded net. Only he could free her
and let her fly . . . straight into his arms.

AVAILABLE NOW: